EastEnders

TIFFANY'S
Secret Diary

The original idea for this book
was conceived by Mal Young, BBC Head of Drama Series

This book is published to accompany the BBC television series *EastEnders*.
Executive Producer: Matthew Robinson

Published by BBC Worldwide Ltd, Woodlands, 80 Wood Lane, London W12 OTT

First published 1998
Copyright © Novelisation Kate Lock 1998
The moral right of the author has been asserted.

ISBN 0 563 55104 6

Editorial Consultant: Jake Lushington
Commissioning Editor: Sue Kerr
Project Editor: Lara Speicher
Copy Editor: Julian Flanders
Book Design: Lisa Pettibone
Cover Design: Town Group Creative/DW Design
Picture Research: Susannah Parker
Script Research: Sharon Batten

Printed and bound in Great Britain by Redwood Books, Trowbridge, Wiltshire
Colour picture sections printed by Lawrence Allen, Weston-super-Mare
Cover printed by Belmont Press Ltd, Northampton

EastEnders

TIFFANY'S
Secret Diary

As seen by Kate Lock

My diary

by Tiffany Raymond (age 19)

Keep Out!

This diary is private and not to be read by anybody!

(unless I end up famous – ha ha!)

18 July 1996

I'm pregnant. I can't believe it. I've been sitting on my bed, looking at this indicator stick thing for the last quarter of an hour, hoping the second pink line will fade. No sign so far. I keep checking the instructions, thinking I must've read them wrong. According to what they say, I'm definitely in the club. It don't seem real. Just because this little window's got a couple of lines on it, me whole future's suddenly up the spout.

I've been feeling rough for a week or so – sick, a bit wobbly, knackered all the time – but I put it down to a bug that's going round, at first anyway. It never even crossed my mind I might be pregnant. I mean, I didn't think I could have children. Not after what happened. I thought me insides were messed up for good. I suppose that's why I weren't more careful. There didn't seem to be no point in taking precautions. I've been going along in me own sweet way, thinking I could get away with it, and now look.

The worst thing is, I don't even know whose it is. I mean, I've been with Tony for five weeks now, so I think it's his. Well, I hope so, because the thought of it being Grant Mitchell's makes me feel even more sick than I do already. We just did it the once. Actually, it's the second time, if you count ten months ago, when I started at the Vic – which you can't, not unless I've got the gestation period of an elephant. It weren't romantic or nothing. First time I did it out of curiosity – well, I like a challenge – but this time it happened because we was both feeling a bit lonely and depressed. We had a couple of drinks, I blubbed into his shirt and the next thing I knew we was having sex on the shag-pile (must be why they call it that, mustn't it?). In the morning we was back to fighting as per usual. He wanted to keep it secret, which was fine by me. As if I'm gonna tell the world and his wife that I slept with Walford's answer to Guy the Gorilla. And believe me, his chest's hairy enough!

Maybe that's why I slept with Tony the next day. He's such a contrast. He was so nervous and inexperienced when it came down to it – practically a virgin – and it was kind of sweet, all that fumbling enthusiasm. Made a change, you know? He's near enough my own age, unlike Grant, who's miles older, and we like the same things – music, dancing, having a good time – although I must admit, his idea of 'recreation' goes too far, even for me. He's been dealing Es with his mate Dan. I want him to stop, but he don't want to know.

God, what a choice – a drug dealer or a thug. My life's falling to pieces here. I've got to tell someone, or I'll go mad. I'm going to find Bianca.

22 July 1996

It's definite. I've been to a family planning clinic and they confirmed it. They assumed I was going to keep it and said things like, 'Is Mum taking her folic acid?' and I looked over my shoulder, wondering who they was talking about. Then I realised they meant me. But I haven't decided whether I want to be a mum or not. I mean, I'm only 19, I've got me whole life ahead of me.

Bianca thinks I should tell Tony, but I'm not sure. I don't want my baby growing up around drugs. On the other hand, I don't think I can go through this on my own... At least Simon's been OK about it. I knew he would be. We've always looked out for each other, ever since Mum left. When it comes down to it, my brother's all the family I've got. I don't count Dad. I never want to see him again.

I suppose Bianca's the closest I've got to a sister. I've known her since I started at Walford High. Funny, innit? We couldn't have been more different then. I was 13, the oldest in the class and wearing me first Wonderbra, and B was this skinny little freckle-faced kid who used to tag along behind. She asked me how she could get a boyfriend and I said, 'Mascara and strawberry-flavour lipgloss', and when Steven Mackie asked her out she thought I was the bees knees. Then we found out we lived near each other and palled up, and we've been mates ever since.

She's the only person I can tell everything. Well, almost everything. There's some stuff in my life she didn't know about, until the other day. When I told her about what me Dad did, pushing me down the stairs like that, and me losing the baby and all the complications, she was really shocked. I think she was a bit hurt, to be honest. She went, 'Tiff, how come you never told me that?' and I said, 'Oh, B, you don't know how much I wanted to,' cos I did. But Dad that made me swear not to say nothing. He said he wouldn't like me to have another accident, and I took the hint.

24 July 1996

Tony knows. I don't know how he feels – I told him at this Seventies night we went to and his face went all funny, but the music was really loud and it was impossible to talk properly. Grant was there, too. He was dancing with this woman, Lorraine, David Wicks's ex-wife. They seemed to be getting on well. I felt odd talking to him, even though I see him every day behind the bar, cos he could be my baby's father.

Hot gossip! Bianca went off with Lenny last night and didn't come back! She and Ricky broke up over scheming Sam Mitchell (another one – they always spell trouble) and Ricky went off in a huff to Manchester to stay with Frank. I don't blame her. I know she's really still in love with Ricky, but, like I said to her, love don't count for nothing in my book.

30 July 1996

Been back to the clinic for more advice. Got to make up my mind, fast, if I'm not gonna keep it. I'm more confused than ever. Tony says he'll support me – he's got quite into the idea and keeps fussing round me, bringing me cups of tea in bed and stuff – but I just don't know if I'm ready to have a kid. Then again, with my medical history, it could be the only chance I'll ever get.

2 August 1996

I went to see Kathy and her baby yesterday, hoping it might help me make up my mind (although I didn't tell her about me being pregnant). Ben's really gorgeous. I held him in my arms and he was peeping up at me and smiling, which suddenly freaked me out. The thought of holding my own baby like that made me want to cry and I had to give him back. I'm very weepy these days – even those ads for baked beans set me off. Kathy and Phil've really been through it with Ben, he had meningitis and he's deaf in one ear. She said being a mother means making sacrifices and that you can never know if you've made the right decision. Some help!

5 August 1996

Awful morning sickness today – I was in and out of the loo, puking up. Peggy said I was as white as a sheet and sent me home. She reckoned I'd got one of them 24-hour bugs. Grant's been looking at me a bit suss, though. Don't know how much longer I can go on keeping this a secret, especially since Tony's kid sister Sarah knows. She came round to the flat looking for him, caught me hurling and guessed the rest. Being a religious nut, she started going on about how Tony had to marry me. Next thing I know, she's bent his ear and he comes back to give me grief. We had a blazing row and he admitted he's scared of commitment. So I ain't holding my breath about a fairytale ending. Still don't know if I'm even gonna keep it yet...

2 September 1996

What a week! I've been to Blackpool with Tony, Simon, Sarah, Bianca, Joe (B's half-brother), Dan and his girlfriend, Mel. We went to a club and Dan and Tony started dealing, which made me furious. I told him that since he couldn't be bothered to behave responsibly, he obviously didn't want this child and that I was going to have an abortion. You know what? He didn't even bother to try and talk me out of it. It hurt me so much because, deep down inside, I want to have this kid.

We didn't sleep together that night and I wouldn't speak to him all the next day. Went to a club again that night. Sarah started acting weird and collapsed on the dance floor. It turned out Dan had put an E in her drink, which had given her a bad trip. She went running out and nearly got knocked down by a car, and we all chased her to the beach.

When Tony found out what had happened, he threw the rest of the pills away and said he was finished with dealing. Dan was mad at him, but I was really pleased. I tried to talk to him but he went off somewhere. B and I caught up with him eventually, sitting on a bench with Simon. I told him I wanted us to be together and that I would keep the baby. I could tell he was relieved.

Tony's been really nice since we got back and has promised to find a proper job. I feel much happier about things now. It's such a relief to have made up my mind. I know it's the right decision. Maybe things won't be so bad after all.

5 September 1996

Tony and Simon ain't getting on, and I don't know why. Simon's being bitchy about him and when I ask Tony what's going on, he just clams up. Oh well, I'm not gonna worry about them. Simon's a big boy now, he can fight his own battles. I'm just glad he got shot of that bullying boyfriend of his, Howard. He was a really nasty piece of work. I told him to sling his hook when he came back recently and he shoved me against a table. It really hurt and I had some bleeding. I was worried I might lose the baby, but Tony took me for a check-up and they said everything was fine. Thank goodness!

I can't imagine how I'd feel if I lost the baby now. I actually bought a pregnancy book today. It was really interesting. The baby's fully formed already. My tummy's getting rounder now, though you wouldn't spot it unless you knew. Fortunately, busybody Peggy is away at the moment, on holiday in New Zealand with her new boyfriend, George. Grant's brought Lorraine in to work behind the bar with us. She seems OK – got him to organise a Caribbean night at the Vic. Bianca's Carmen Miranda outfit was a scream. I think she had half Mark Fowler's stall on her head!

12 September 1996

I'm living in the Vic now, with Grant. It's a long story. I hardly know where to start. I'll go back to the beginning, Monday. Grant had got wind of me being pregnant – he heard Tony mouthing off about it in the bar apparently – and kept going on about it, asking if it was his. I said, 'If it comes out with two horns and a forked tail, who knows, it could be yours,' joking like, but he wouldn't let it drop, so I said it was Tony's. Thing is, I let it slip that I'm three months gone and he just put two and two together. He was waiting for me when I finished my shift and followed me into the Square. He was really intense – different, sort of vulnerable-looking – and I ended up admitting that it might be his, but that he didn't have a look-in because me and Tony were together.

But that was before I went home and walked in on my so-called boyfriend kissing my so-called brother. I couldn't believe my eyes. I just turned and ran, crying my eyes out. Of course, Grant heard me and wanted to know what was going on. Then Tony and Simon turned up to talk things over and I wanted to hurt them so much that I told Grant I'd been lying and that it was his baby, definitely.

He took me back to the Vic and was really sweet, offering to let me stay for the night in his room and he would have the sofa. I couldn't think where else to go at that time of night, so I went along with it, thinking I'd break the truth to him later. When he said, 'Why didn't you tell me about the baby?' I had to think fast, so I said, 'I didn't think you'd be interested. You're hardly the fatherly type.' He looked all upset and went, 'I've wanted a kid for years. I was so jealous of Phil having Ben.' He said he wanted to stand by me, and even when I pointed out that this is the twentieth century and blokes don't have to do that no more, he still weren't put off. He took my hand and stared into my eyes and said, 'I want you to keep it. I want us to keep it.' It was such a relief to have this big, strong bloke being all protective, especially as he admitted that he'd always quite liked me. I went up to bed and when he came in to say goodnight I asked him to stay. We lay together on the bed and he cuddled me and stroked my tummy and I felt so safe and that's when I started to think, well, maybe this could work...

When Peggy found out about the baby, she went bananas and accused me of trying to trap her precious son. I gave as good as I got and told her I was carrying her future grandchild, which brought her up short, but she made it clear she wasn't happy about me being there anyway.

Tony came round in the morning and had a row with Grant, insisting it was his baby. Grant chucked him out, but he put me on the spot afterwards, asking how come I was so certain the baby was his? I had to improvise, so I said it was because me and Tony hadn't really done anything – as in going all the way – because of him being gay, which I hadn't known about until I found him snogging Simon. But that seemed to convince him.

16 September 1996
Still not talking to Simon or Tony. I feel totally betrayed by my brother and I'm not gonna forgive him. I told B what happened and she was gobsmacked, though to be honest, I'm not sure

which bit shocked her the most – the news that they're both gay, or the fact that I've moved in with Grant – who is on a level with the Antichrist as far as she's concerned. Ricky has come back from Frank's and he and B have made up and now they're planning the biggest wedding Walford's ever seen. True love conquers all, eh? Still not sure what B sees in Ricky – I mean, I'd hardly call him a catch. I'd've thrown him back if it were me! Still, so long as he makes her happy…

It's really crowded upstairs at the Vic. Besides me and Grant and Peggy, Lorraine has got the spare room. I could do without her hanging about all the time – she's really nosy about the baby, and keeps telling me to go to antenatal check-ups and stuff. She and Grant nag me about taking care of myself as if they're my parents. For heaven's sake!

30 September 1996

Apparently Dad's in hospital with pancreatitis. He can rot in his bed for all I care. He's a drunk and if his organs are so pickled that they're packing up, he's only got himself to blame. I don't see how he can possibly expect any sympathy after what he did to us. I mean, he used to beat Simon, and although he never actually hit me, he was vicious in other ways. When he found out about me and Mr Sykes, my English teacher, he shouted, 'You're a whore, just like your mother.' I said, 'I don't blame Mum for leaving a useless no-hoper like you,' and he shoved me really hard and that's when I fell down the stairs. After that I didn't need Mr Sykes's money for an abortion.

It was Dad who said I'd be damaged inside. He used to go on and on about it being my punishment for being 'a slag'. I believed him. About my tubes not working, I mean. I'm not a slag – God, I hate that word! – I just know the value of things. If you've got it, flaunt it, that's my motto. And make sure the bloke shows his appreciation by the bulge in his wallet, as well as his trousers.

Well, that's how I used to be anyway, when I was footloose and fancy free. I could wind men round me little finger. Now, my jeans are getting tighter by the day and I'm beginning to feel old and staid already. I was gonna have such a bright, glamorous future – marry a rich bloke (preferably one with a yacht and houses all round the world), leave crummy old Walford far behind. When I remember how I used to be when I came back to the Square last year, I feel as if I'm a different person.

3 October 1996

Had some funny sharp twinges in my stomach the other day. Grant went into panic mode and rushed me round to Dr Legg's, who said it was probably just an abdominal spasm. He's arranging for me to have an early scan, just to be on the safe side.

Ran into Tony today. He asked how I knew the baby wasn't his. I told him I just did. I can't stop wondering whether Tony knew he was gay when he was with me or not. I mean, I had no idea, and I usually have an instinct for these things. When I asked him, he said he still wasn't sure and that he might be bisexual. Pur-lease! Either you is or you ain't in my book.

7 October 1996

It's a girl! Amazing! I'm having a daughter! Had the scan today and everything's absolutely fine. Grant came with me, and when they said would we like to know what sex the baby was, we looked at each other and said yes. They took some pictures of her – I've got one in front of me now. Hello, little baby! She's so cute and you can see so much detail – her nose, her fingers, her toes. She's even sucking her thumb in one of them. That blew me right away.

Grant's face was a study. I thought he was gonna cry. I felt pretty close to it, too. It was an incredibly emotional moment, seeing our baby kicking and moving inside me, and the little heart beating away so fast. It brought me and Grant closer together. I suddenly felt that we might really be able to make a go of bringing her up together. Not just the practical stuff, but properly, as parents. Grant's got a side to him that nobody else sees. He can be very tender and caring. We get on much better these days and I'm beginning to feel quite fond of him. I don't think it's love – not yet, anyway – but who knows?

Afterwards, we went home via Mothercare and Grant bought up half the store. Well, I'm exaggerating, but we did get some gorgeous newborn baby clothes and the diddiest pair of trainers you've ever seen, plus some maternity dresses for me, which are quite presentable. I mean, they're not high fashion, but at least they're not smocks or tents. I'm determined to keep looking my best!

8 October 1996

I can't believe it! Ian Beale's been shot, right here, just down the road. They think it was some drive-by shooting. Grant's been up at the hospital with Phil and Kathy and Cindy, Ian's wife. What a nightmare it must be for her…

21 October 1996

It gets worse. Grant thinks Cindy was behind the shooting. She's done a bunk to France with two of their kids. Ian's in a terrible state, and Grant's going mad, ranting about David Wicks, who he says was having an affair with Cindy. I don't know why he's got so involved. I mean, it's his brother's problem really. Phil's Kathy's wife and Ian's her son. But Grant seems really obsessed about it.

25 October 1996

Dad turned up at the Vic yesterday. He came storming in and went berserk, shouting at me and calling me names, just like the other time. It was such a shock. Then, all of a sudden, I got this really weird sensation like I'd been socked in the guts and I felt quite winded. It made me double up, but Lorraine thought it was just the baby kicking. Well, my baby certainly didn't think much of her first introduction to her grandad, poor little love!

It certainly freaked me. I had such a terrifying feeling of having been there before. Grant threw him out and I went to lie down, just as a precaution. Later, Grant came upstairs and was really concerned, stroking my hair and holding me. It felt so right, so good, and one thing led to another. Before I knew it, we were making love. He was very gentle and sweet. I really think he could be the one. How funny that I never saw it up till now! He was right under me nose all the time...

5 November 1996

Fireworks all round. Lorraine has moved Joe into the Vic to keep an eye on him because he's behaving so weird. Next thing I hear, he's covered himself in lighter fuel and is running around playing with matches, babbling about Grant being evil. Lorraine rang David, who managed to get the matches off him, but I don't need that kind of stress going on in my life, not after the incident with Dad. It's not good for the baby. Poor Peggy (words I never thought I'd write, but we're getting on better these days) has been acting funny as well, and now I know why. She confessed to me she's found a lump in her breast. I told her to go and see Dr Legg straight away, but she didn't seem keen on the idea. She made me swear not to say anything to Grant or Phil. I hope she's alright.

Now for the good news. Grant has asked if I want to go for a short break to Paris! I didn't need asking twice, but I told him no sightseeing. I said, 'I'm not walking up thousands of stairs in my condition.' He said, 'What about clothes shops?' cos he knows what I'm like, and I goes, 'That's different.' I love it when he spoils me!

Left my diary at home, so I couldn't keep this up while we were away. There's a lot to catch up on. For starters, I'm no longer Tiffany Raymond. I'm Tiffany Mitchell! I still can't get used to it. 'Mrs Mitchell' sounds like Peggy, not me...

We got married in Gibraltar on the 19th, after Grant proposed to me in Paris. We were walking along the Seine one evening, talking about when the baby comes and what I'm gonna do and how he's going to help, and he suddenly said, 'We could always get married, of course.' I was really shocked – I mean, he didn't even stop walking or anything – and I said, 'Grant Mitchell, are you proposing to me?' Then he stopped and took my hand and his face was dead serious and he went, 'Tiffany, would you do me the honour of being my wife?' My insides went all gooey and I got this tingle down my spine and I said something really stupid like, 'Do you really mean it?' He just kept looking at me with that intense expression and I knew then that I did love him and that I couldn't think of anything better than marrying him. So I said yes. I just didn't realise he meant right away!

Later, the penny dropped that he must have been planning it all along because he'd brought our birth certificates and his divorce papers and all that with him from England, and he said he knew we could get married in Gibraltar. So that's when we decided to extend our holiday. We had to fill in about ten million forms and Grant got a bit narked by all the paperwork. But we got there in the end and tied the knot in a registry office with a couple of army blokes that Grant knew as witnesses. Afterwards, we stayed in this posh hotel and we spent the night in the bridal suite, which had a jacuzzi and all, and Grant had this enormous bunch of roses delivered for me (although he wouldn't let me drink champagne, the meanie).

It was nice. Simple, but nice. And of course, we didn't have all the hassle of organising a great big do with loads of guests.

I'd always thought I'd have a big white wedding, three-tier wedding cake, designer dress, the works (pictures in 'Hello!') and a bit of me's secretly sad that it didn't happen that way. But then being swept off your feet like that's romantic too, isn't it? Bianca kept going on about 'didn't I feel I'd missed out?' when I told her, but I said no, I liked it like that. Anyway, she's miffed that I beat her to it!

Peggy had a few things to say and all when Grant and me walked into the Vic and he calmly announced that I was his wife. She's been making comments about how her boys were brought up to respect family and marriage, as if she thinks I'm gonna let Grant down. I told her I knew it wasn't going to be easy, but that I really cared for Grant – which is true – and that I'm going to do everything I can to make it work. She calmed down then. Simon was pretty gobsmacked too. He said he'd tell Tony for me. I don't feel mad about those two any more – I just think Tony's lucky to have a good bloke like Simon. Funny how it all worked out for the best in the end, isn't it?

4 December 1996

Grant went ballistic yesterday because I had a tiny sip of Bianca's vodka and orange. He went for me in front of every-one in the pub, calling me stupid and accusing me of putting the baby at risk. It was so humiliating. He made me cry. Sometimes he treats me like I haven't got any feelings at all. I told him, 'You treat me like I'm some sort of incubator for your baby,' and went off upstairs. I mean, it's always 'the baby this' and 'the baby that' – we've been married less than a month and suddenly I feel like I'm rent-a-womb, not a newly-wed. I love this baby as much as he does and I'm not going to do anything to harm her, but Grant's OTT about her. It worries me what he'll be like when she's born if this is how he is now.

He came up later and sort of apologised and we arranged to go out that evening. Then he remembered he was playing snooker with Phil, so I said I'd come along too, but that didn't go down well. To be honest, I don't think he wanted me there – he's got these ideas about what pregnant women should and shouldn't do – but I called his bluff and he had to keep his promise. Then this bloke started trying to chat me up and Grant flipped and would've smacked him one if Phil hadn't stopped him. After that he gave me the silent treatment all the way home, like it was my fault. Needless to say, we slept back to back last night and woke up in a right frosty atmosphere.

I don't know what changed his mind, but he was much nicer to me later, telling me he's setting up a joint account that I can draw from, which he refused to do when I asked him about it before. I guess that's his way of saying sorry. Words aren't exactly his strong point. Well, you know what they say, actions speak louder and all that. But I wish we could talk about things without World War Three breaking out every time.

Peggy's in a right old state. She had a biopsy at the hospital today and she was taking it out on me something chronic. They called her back in to give her the results. Eventually we got a cab up there because I knew she really wanted some support, whatever she said. The bad news is, she's got breast cancer. Poor Peggy.

9 December 1996

Grant had another go at me today. He thinks I'm trying to be top dog at the Vic instead of Peggy, or something like that. The truth is, I'm just trying to cover for her – she still won't tell them about her having cancer. Course, it ended up with me and Grant having a row. I said that eventually, I'd like us to move out from the Vic and live our own lives – perhaps run a pub of our own, or even something classier, like a wine bar. And he says, 'Leave the Vic? Forget it.' And, not only that, but he expects me to give up working behind the bar after Christmas. That's not anything we've discussed before. I feel absolutely fine. I don't need to lie about for the next three months – I'll go mad with boredom. But would he listen? No way. Talk about being a prisoner in your own home...

12 December 1996

When I told B that Grant expects me to live like some meek little mouse, hiding away upstairs and knitting bootees, she said she'd come over and cheer me up. We were gonna have a girls' night in with just the two of us, but then Ricky wanted to come, and Huw and Lenny heard, and somehow it ended up as a party. I was a bit worried about the noise, but it was just a bit of fun and no one was causing any trouble or nothing and it was actually really nice for me to have some mates round.

Sometimes, living with Grant, I feel as if I'm becoming old before my time. I mean, I'm 20 and he's 14 years older than me. Now I like older men, I always have. Generally speaking, they treat you better and they're better in bed and they're better off, too, plus they're more appreciative. But when it comes down to things like taste in music and clothes, they haven't got a clue! Grant's a bit like that. He knows nothing about dance music, he probably thinks Jamiroquai is some sort of curry, and his trainers are about ten years out of date. What I'm saying is that, although I love him, there's some things – well, quite a lot of things – we can't share. That's why it's important to me to let my hair down once in a while with friends my own age.

Anyway, Grant got wind of the party and came storming upstairs. I was holding an empty beer can that I'd picked up off the stereo and, of course, he immediately assumed I'd been drinking. Next thing, he was booting everybody out and yelling at me, without even bothering to listen to what I had to say. It was like the other night in the bar, only he was even nastier than before. Something in me snapped and I started screaming back at him about what a pig he was, and then I ran out after Bianca and Ricky.

I spent the night on B's sofa, which isn't exactly comfortable when you're six months' gone. I've got quite a bump now. I was determined not to go back until Grant apologised, which he did, this morning. I told him he had to give me more space and he can't carry on like some Victorian husband, laying down the law. Also, I wanted to go out with my mates more and I wanted him to make an effort to get along with them. He agreed (a bit reluctantly) and, in return, I promised not to drink. We called a truce and I went back to the Vic, though B thought I was mad.

Peggy caused another upset later when she finally told Phil and Grant about the cancer (she's going in for a lumpectomy on Monday). When Grant realised I'd been supporting her, he forgave me for not telling him and actually said I'd behaved very responsibly! Should I have got that in writing, do you think?

23 December 1996

I've gone and done something really stupid. I told Lorraine that the baby might not be Grant's. It all came out after a night at the Cobra Club. I got Grant to agree to come so that he could meet my mates, but the whole thing was a disaster. I had a drink – just one, a cocktail, and it was mostly fruit juice anyway – and Grant saw me with it and chucked a mental. I told him to lighten up, it's nearly Christmas. I was just trying to get into the spirit of it and it's not as if one little drink's going to hurt. But he practically dragged me out, embarrassing me again in front of everybody. Personally, I think the real reason he gets so worked up is because he can't stand seeing me enjoy myself. Well, I soon put him straight on that point, telling him I wasn't gonna change my life just because I'm having a baby. If he didn't go on and on about it so much, I might actually slow down, but his attitude just makes me want to do it more. It's the only way to show him I'm not just a kind of grow-bag for his kid.

We got back to the Vic and had a right royal row and I ended up threatening to leave. That was when he got really violent. It was scary. He just seemed to lose control and started shaking me, shouting, 'You ain't going anywhere!' I don't know what he might have done if Lorraine hadn't heard and come in and stopped him.

She was really kind and stayed with me after Grant left. I told her what had happened and that's when it all came out. I didn't mean it to. It's just that she was so sympathetic and under-standing. I could see she was shocked. She went on about how lies can wreck a marriage and that it would be better to tell Grant the truth now, before the baby's born. In the end, I agreed. I mean, in my heart of hearts, I know it's the right thing to do. I always meant to tell him, but I'm terrified of how he'll react.

The next morning he apologised and admitted he was really frightened of something going wrong with the baby because he wanted it so much, which was why he went off the deep end. I tried to tell him then, but we got interrupted, and after that I just never found the right moment. Bianca thinks there's no point in rocking the boat – after all, it could be Grant's – and that what he don't know can't hurt him. I think she's got a good point. Besides, I don't fancy being pregnant and homeless over Christmas! But now I can't get Lorraine off my back and she keeps asking if I've done it yet. Wish I'd never opened me big mouth.

25 December 1996

Merry Christmas Tiffany. You poor cow. What have you got yourself into? You're married into a family of nutcases. I'm here at Tony and Simon's, having a nice time, eating crisps and watching telly in front of the fire. We're having a laugh, which is more than they'll be doing over at the Vic.

I just had to get out. Peggy's big family Christmas lunch bombed. It was so bad, it was funny, looking back on it.

Everyone was there, sitting round this long table in the bar – Phil, Kathy, Ted (Tony's dad, he's Kathy's brother), George, Lorraine, Joe, Peggy, Grant and me. Grant had been having digs at me all morning because I went out to a party last night and came back late. I just ignored his sarky comments, which of course wound him up even more. Then George – who announced he and Peggy was getting married, by the way – asked if I'd like some wine, and I said yes, mostly to get back at Grant. It was Joe who really stirred things up, telling Lorraine not to give Grant the carving knife because he had the mark of the devil on him! Phil, who was plastered, thought that was hilarious, and he and Lorraine had a row and then everybody else started joining in. Then Joe went, 'If Tiffany is Grant's wife, right, why was he kissing my mum?' and everyone was silent. Lorraine looked really awkward but Grant said it was a Christmas kiss under the mistletoe. Joe kept going on about Grant 'comforting' her, but I didn't really believe him. I mean, Joe is definitely one sandwich short of a picnic. All the same, it made me cross and I told George to give me a top-up, and that was when all hell broke loose. Finally, I said to Peggy, 'You're right, being with your family at Christmas is important. If anyone wants me, I'll be with mine,' and walked out with my head held high. And do you know, I feel pretty good about it.

26 December 1996
Grant came over to apologise this afternoon. I knew he would. We both agreed to try harder to make the marriage work and now I'm back at the Vic again. Eating a lot of cold turkey.

30 December 1996
I really thought Grant was making an effort. He booked us a table at this swanky restaurant and we were having a good time, then it all started to fall apart and I'm not sure why. I said

I was looking forward to us having a place of our own one day – I mean, the Vic's so crowded, it's not as if it's a place I can call my own, is it? And I'll never be able to do things my way while Peggy rules the roost. Not to mention having that stick-insect Lorraine and her barmy son in tow. I said, perhaps then me and Grant could be a real family, but he didn't seem to know what I was going on about, and started having a go at me again. He's got no idea how he belittles me, sometimes. It's like I'm nobody to him. If I'd had any idea what marriage to him was going to be like, I'd have jumped in the blooming Seine and swum to safety when he proposed to me in Paris.

2 January 1997

'Let's try really hard to make 1997 a good year for the three of us,' I said to Grant on New Year's Eve. I remember it distinctly because I really meant it – a fresh start for him and me and the baby. I was so sick of all the argy-bargy we've been having. I'm sure fighting and screaming at each other doesn't do the baby any good. They can hear what's going on in the womb, you know. I read in a magazine that if you watch a TV show regularly, they even get to know the theme tune, so it stands to reason they know when their mummy and daddy's arguing. Anyway, Grant agreed, which I was relieved about, and we got on with decorating the Vic for this big party Peggy was throwing in the evening.

Then along comes Lorraine and has another go at me when Grant's out of the room. She got this sort of pained look on her face, like she's the one really suffering, and I knew what she was gonna say straight away. I told her I was fed up with her interfering and I wasn't gonna risk my marriage on the off-chance Grant wasn't the father and that if she couldn't hack it then she'd better do everyone a favour and move out.

Well, it must've sunk in because later on that night she came over to me in the middle of the party and said she was leaving.

She had the nerve to mention Grant and the baby again, which made me see red and I ended up shouting at her, which Grant noticed. I told him she was just being bitchy, but it must've made him suspicious. Course, I didn't imagine Lorraine would give the game away, did I? The clock had just struck midnight, and everybody was cheering and drinking champagne and I saw Grant coming over and said, 'Happy New Year' and kissed him. He got hold of me and yanked me out the bar and up the stairs. I was annoyed but I still didn't guess what was coming. He said, 'You've been lying. I know about the baby,' and then my heart sank cos I knew this was crunch time. I tried to make out it was that cow Lorraine who was lying, but he wouldn't have it. He grabbed hold of me by the shoulders and started shaking me so hard my teeth was rattling in my head and I couldn't speak.

Luckily Nigel came in at that moment – he seemed really upset about something – and I bolted while I had the chance. I told Bianca I needed to get out the Vic right away, and she and Ricky took me back to their place. Grant guessed and he came round, hammering on the door so hard I thought he was going to break it down. B told him to sod off but he just barged straight in and demanded to talk to me. I knew there was no getting away from it, so I decided to tell him the truth, hoping he might understand if I explained why I'd lied.

He was so, so cold. His eyes were like chips of ice. He said, 'All I want you to do is get the baby tested. If it's mine, then I'm having it. If it ain't, you can drop it in the canal for all I care.' Then he went to walk out and I said, 'But what about me?' and – God, it's really hard to write this, I'm crying now, just thinking about it – he said, 'I don't want you Tiffany, I never have. All I ever wanted was the baby.'

So that's it. I'm still at B's. My marriage is over. I'm totally depressed, a complete mess, can't stop blubbing. What's gonna become of us now, little one? My poor, innocent baby, you haven't done anything to deserve this. I can feel you moving inside me as I write – there you go, a kick (Hi there!). You're growing by the day, getting ready to come into the big, wide world, and what have I got to offer you? Nothing. No, there is something. My love. For what it's worth. Grant didn't want it, so I'm all yours, baby.

6 January 1997

Grant won't have anything to do with me now. It's all Lorraine's fault. If only she'd kept her trap shut, I'd never be in this mess. I can't believe she would drop me in it like that. I mean, she goes on a bit sometimes, but basically I thought she was my friend.

Peggy came round today, wanting to get the inside story. When I told her the truth about the baby, she blew her top and called me a stupid little tart. She calmed down when I told her how sorry I was (and how!) for misleading Grant, and that I really wanted it to be his kid. I know she does, too. She's got granny-mania, has Peggy. I think she's on my side.

13 January 1997

B's given me a job working on her stall. I'm standing around in the freezing cold, me fingers stiff with cold and me nose turning into an icicle, trying to sell dresses to people who should know better. Trouble is, I just can't be bothered with Bianca's fancy sales talk. If something don't suit someone, I tell 'em. B's not very happy about it, but I reckon I'm doing them a favour.

16 January 1997

Now I know why Lorraine ratted on me. She wanted Grant for herself. I'm amazed I didn't suss out her little scheme. There she was, pretending to be all concerned and preaching to me about honesty, while all the time she was having it off with him. The two-faced bitch. Bianca told me the score. She said she'd seen

Joe earlier and he told her Grant and his mum were nuts about each other and that I didn't have a look-in. Even then, I didn't really believe it – I mean, Joe's off with the fairies half the time – but I had to find out for myself. I went straight round to the Vic and there was no sign of either of them, so I went upstairs and found Grant and Lorraine, sitting on the sofa, as cosy as you like. And you know the worst bit? He didn't even bother to deny it. He just settled back, put his arm around her, and said, 'Yeah, it's true, so what?' really rubbing my nose in it. I said, 'How dare you make me feel guilty about lying to you when all the time you was cheating on me?' and he got really angry and threw me out.

20 January 1997

I'm not taking any more of this. I can't stand living on Grant's doorstep and seeing Lorraine swanning about with him. I mean, he's still my husband. It hurts, it really hurts. And do you know what she had the nerve to do? Come round here, saying she wanted to apologise. Amazing, isn't it? What do you say when you've done what she's done? 'I'm really sorry I swiped your bloke and smashed up your life and ruined your baby's chances of having a decent upbringing, but you can't have him back cos I've got him?'

Only she didn't, of course. She waffled on about how bad she felt and how she never expected all this to happen. Well, what did she thing was gonna happen? It only goes to prove she doesn't know Grant like I do. Least I know the bad stuff as well as the good. I think he's been putting on some kind of front with her. I bet she's got no idea what he's capable of. He won't keep up his goody two-shoes act for long. That woman's in for a nasty shock and I for one won't be feeling any sympathy for her when she finds out.

Anyway, I've made a decision. I'm going to get out of Walford. Thank God for our joint account! I went to the bank today and cleared it out. I've got eight hundred quid, which should see me alright for a while. I'm gonna go to Spain and see me mates in Marbella. We used to have a right laugh when I was out there working, and that's what I need right now. I might even stay out there, who knows?

3 March 1997

Got back a week ago. I didn't write me diary in Spain, just didn't feel like it. Too relaxed, I think. It was so good to escape from Albert Square and just chill out. I've done nothing but sit in the sun with me feet up. I got a bit lonely after a while cos my friends all had to work, so I called Bianca and she came over for a bit. To be honest, I got a bit panicky about the baby. I had to come home because they won't let you fly any later than 31 or 32 weeks, and even then I had to lie because I'm a lot further gone than that.

I'm staying with Tony and Simon again, till we can get things sorted one way or the other – well, OK, until we find out who the baby's father is. The way Tony's acting, fussing round me like a mother hen, you'd think we was married, not me and Grant (who ain't even said hello to me since I've been back). Simon seems to be cool about it. He says all three of us can bring the baby up together.

I'm trying to believe it'll be alright, but inside I'm so scared. I've got no money, no prospects, no home and I don't know the first thing about looking after babies. The flat's tiny enough as it is, and that's before there's baby clothes drying everywhere and toys and nappies all over the place. Plus, there's so much she'll need and it costs a bomb. I get so depressed that I don't go down the shops no more because I can't afford any of it. I don't see how we'll all manage on Simon's job on the stall and Tony's giro. I know I should be grateful – I mean, at least I've got a roof over my head – but I can't stop thinking how things could be, especially when I see Grant. Then I see Lorraine and my heart sinks... I was hoping they might have split up while I was away, but I ran into them the moment I got back, arms all around each other. Talk about sticking the knife in and twisting it. I know it's stupid, but I still love him.

4 March 1997

I went to see Grant today, to ask him to sign this form I got from the DSS which means I can claim more maternity benefit. He was so horrible to me, just blanked me out the way he does sometimes and curled his lip in disgust. He really hates me. He told me he wasn't nothing to do with me no more and he wasn't gonna lift a finger to help, but in the end I got Peggy to sign it. She's being really great, bless her.

10 March 1997

I'm as fat as a pig. Sanjay's mum said there was nothing so beautiful as the sight of a heavily pregnant woman, but I reckon she must need glasses. Nelly the Elephant's got nothing on me. Bianca says I'm not fat, I'm blooming. 'Yeah – blooming awful!' I told her.

Baby's overdue now and I'm really fed up with waiting. My ankles are swollen, my back's killing me and I just can't get comfortable in bed whichever way I lie. Had a nap this afternoon, then B came round. We had a chat and she made me some tea and tried to cheer me up. I think she's sussed how I really feel about Grant, but I lied and said all I wanted from him was money.

Simon and Tony have gone out to the club. Tony wanted to stay in with me but I said I'd ring them if anything happened. I've got me hospital bag all packed, and things don't move that fast with first babies, anyway. I'm trying not to think about being in labour. Don't know how I'm gonna cope. Just the thought of the pain terrifies me. I haven't got anybody to hold my hand and help me through it. God, I wish me mum was here. I need you, Mum. Oh, no, I'm crying again, it's making the ink run. I'm pathetic, a total wreck.

Later: Peggy's just been to see how I am, which was sweet of her. She reckons Lorraine's a fling and Grant'll get tired of her. Apparently, they've been rowing a lot recently. I told her that Grant hates me, but she said he's just reacting the only way he knows and that he did it to Sharon too. Peggy thinks that he might change his mind when he sees the baby. I hope so.

16 March 1997

Well, I've had it – a little girl, weighing 7lbs 12oz. She's sleeping in her carrycot beside me now, mouth all puckered up and arms thrown out to the sides. She's a doll. I can't get over it. My baby. I get such a thrill out of saying that. Haven't got a name for her yet, though I'm working on a few ideas. Perhaps I'll keep this diary for you, little one, write about what you've been doing and how you're growing and all the stuff you and me do together, and then one day, when you're older, you'll have something to look back on.

She came the night of my last diary entry. Not long after I'd finished writing the doorbell rang and when I went to open it, there was Grant. He asked if he could come in and I thought, right, I'm gonna go for it and tell him how I really feel. So I told him I missed him and he said he didn't want to rehash old ground and that he wanted a divorce. Just like that. I was completely stunned. It was like he'd hit me in the face. I mean, I thought, for a second, he'd come because he cared, because he wanted to see me. Turns out he wants to marry Lorraine.

Well, we had an almighty row and I told him he could whistle for his divorce cos I wasn't gonna give it him. He went out into the Square and I followed him. By this time, I was pretty hysterical and I just let rip and started to hit him. Next thing I knew, I'd slipped over and there was this pain in my stomach and I couldn't move, it was so strong. I realised it was a contraction, but I didn't expect it to be so fierce. Looking back, I might have been having some earlier cos my tummy was really griping. Anyway, I said, 'Grant, the baby's coming. You've gotta take me to the hospital.' I was in agony and I begged him to stay with me. He did, and I was so relieved.

The contractions got worse and worse on the way to the hospital and it took them ages to give me an epidural. I was getting more and more tired and eventually they put me on a drip to speed things up. I was pushing for what seemed like hours and still nothing happened and by then I was exhausted. A doctor came in and they looked at the monitor and said the baby had gone into distress and I needed an emergency caesarean. I was so frightened, I started screaming, 'I want my baby, I want my baby,' and they wheeled me off to theatre really quickly. I was almost out of it by then, what with all the drugs. I couldn't feel a thing and I had no idea what was going on. They put a screen up over my stomach so we couldn't see them operate. I felt this tugging sensation and that's when they got her out. The last thing I remember was Grant's face, so pale and tense, and his eyes were bleak, and I thought, 'I've lost her, she's dead,' and then I passed out.

When I came round, Grant was sitting beside me, holding the baby. He said, 'She's fine,' and I could hardly believe it. He gave her to me so gently and I held her in my arms and the tears were rolling down my face. She was so perfect. She's got masses of tufty dark hair and a tiny snub nose and gorgeous blue eyes. I took one look at her and knew she was Grant's. He did too. I could tell by his expression, though he wouldn't admit it, of course. When he put her down in the cot, he whispered, 'There's my girl,' thinking I hadn't heard. But...then he says it's too late for us and that he loves Lorraine, not me.

He promised to come back later with my bag, but Tony brought it instead. He and Simon and Bianca arrived with a bottle of champagne. I haven't seen Grant since. I know he

26

Me looking particularly glam on my 20th birthday. You'd never guess I'd just found out I was pregnant from this sultry pic . . . never in a million years did I think I'd end up with Grant!

Ahhh, early days. This was taken soon after I started working as a barmaid in the Vic. What a sweet, innocent young thing I look! Grant's putting on the big boss act, but I soon had him wrapped around my little finger.

This was me first day behind the bar. Peggy said the takings went up overnight. I always said I was good on the pull – men or pints!

Me and my bro,
Simon. I was
really pleased
when he moved in
with me and Tony
– until he pinched
my boyfriend.

Bianca and me at Blackpool
pleasure beach, 1996, on that
fateful holiday.

Simon trying to persuade me to leave Grant, for the umpteenth time.

Tony really wanted to be the baby's dad, but the blood tests proved otherwise.

Married to the mob: Peggy with her boys, Phil and Grant. Me and Kathy take a back seat, as per usual.

What would I do without B?

Oh dear, that awful dressing gown!!!

Courtney's christening. Proud
parents me and Grant, with
godparents Bianca, Simon
and Phil.

My little girl in her christening
robes. Don't she look gorgeous in
that bonnet?

Grant and I have our marriage blessed in church. Peggy wanted something along the lines of the royal wedding but Grant didn't want a fuss. I was with Peggy! After all, a girl deserves to push the boat out on her special day . . .

The blushing 'bride'. I look quite tasty, though I say it meself!

came back though, cos one of the midwives brought in some flowers and said my husband had just dropped them off. So he must care about me a bit, mustn't he?

17 March 1997

The baby has a name. Courtney. As in Courtney Love, the girl who was married to the singer from Nirvana who topped himself. Lenny came up with it. I said I wanted something wild, but cool and stylish. I originally thought of Janis – after Joplin, you know – but Simon said, 'People aren't gonna think of her, they'll think of Janice Smethurst who works down the butchers on the high street,' and I could see he had a point. Mind you, his names weren't much better. I mean, Eartha? Marlene? Shirley? He says they're all great chanters (or whatever it is the French call them), which I don't doubt, but I had to agree with Bianca, they were all pretty ancient. Plus, I was determined the baby wasn't going to have a name that ended in a 'y', like mine does. I think those names sound fluffy. Blokes always think they can get one over on you with a name like that. Course, Bianca pointed out that Courtney ends in a 'y', but somehow it don't sound girly, it sounds like, 'don't mess with me', and that's what I want for my daughter. You gotta watch out for number one in this world and I'm gonna make sure she knows how to handle herself, so she don't make the same mistakes that I've made.

Listen to me! I'm only 20 myself. Do you know, Courtney, I feel as if I've suddenly aged about ten years, with what you just put me through! But I wouldn't have it any other way. I love being a mum. So far, it's been a doddle. She just eats and sleeps, while I sit here stuffing choccies and being waited on hand and foot by Tony. It's great!

24 March 1997

I've decided to get the blood tests done, like Grant wants. I'm positive Courtney is his, and once he knows it too, that changes everything, don't it? Can't stop now as I've gotta go round to B's. She's really upset because of what Ricky's done. Well, we don't know for sure it was Ricky, but Sarah's been raped, and he was seen running out of the house with a dirty great scratch on his face. I can't believe it of Ricky – like I said to Simon, he's brainless but he ain't exactly dangerous. It's more likely they was having a fling behind B's back. It's not as if he ain't done it before. Remember Sam Mitchell?

3 April 1997

Big day today. Went to the clinic with Tony and Courtney for the DNA tests. Just as were getting into the cab, Grant came out the Vic to his car and I could see Lorraine was wishing him good luck. Then she gave him this big kiss, which made me feel sick to watch. How dare she! If Courtney's Grant's baby, it'll be Miss Flat Bum who'll get her marching orders, not me. (She's got no bum to speak of, you know. She's like a dry old twig. I can't think what he sees in her. He always used to tell me he liked something to hold on to.)

It was awful, sitting in the waiting-room, with all of us there. Talk about being able to cut the atmosphere with a knife – you could've sliced it and served it for tea! Then Grant starts on about what arrangements I'm gonna make for Courtney once it's been proved he's the father, and says he wants to get on with the divorce. At a time like that! Tony weren't much better. I was really nervous – I don't like injections and I was feeling really bad about my little baby having to have a big needle stuck in her – and I got fed up with the pair of them.

Anyway, Ricky's off the hook over the Sarah business – turns out she did it with Robbie (willingly! Blimey!) and then freaked out at Ricky when he found her crying (as you would, if you'd done it with Robbie – ugh). Ted went ape when he heard and beat poor old Robbie up and now he's in hospital. But at least Ricky and Bianca are together again and the wedding's back on. Tony was really down in the dumps about Sarah shopping their dad to the police, but he cheered up later cos the 'Gazette' has offered him a three-month trial as a trainee. Good for him. It's about time he got a lucky break.

7 April 1997

Grant made a real fuss of Courtney today when I went out with the pram. It really built my hopes up, until he turned round and said he was filing for divorce on our wedding anniversary. How cruel can you get? Turns out you have to be married for a year before you can get divorced. I'm trying to be positive about it. At least that gives me until November to win him back. I'm starting my diet today. No more choccies! Lorraine may be Miss Flat Bum but I'm Mrs Fat Bum at the moment.

14 April 1997

We had B's hen night in the Vic tonight. Simon and Tony looked after Courtney, as well as Billy, Carol Jackson's littlest. The blokes kidnapped Ricky in a van and dragged him off somewhere. I hate to think what he's doing right now with Grant and Phil in charge of the entertainment. Us girls all had a really good natter and a laugh about men and sex. Lorraine was behind the bar and Peggy kept dropping all these loaded comments about marriage and how you gotta respect it and stick with it, making Lorraine go all red. I was a bit naughty, too, ordering all these different drinks then changing the order and confusing her. Serves the thieving cow right.

15 April 1997

Bianca and Ricky's wedding day. It was all a bit hairy – Ricky only just made it to the church at the last minute and B was going frantic. He had bits of straw sticking to him and he smelt like a farmyard. Gawd knows where he'd been.

But B looked so beautiful in her dress, I welled up the moment I set eyes on her. I guess it made me think about what I missed out on, getting married so quickly without any fuss. Well, not just that. I mean, it's obvious those two adore each other. Whatever's happened in the past, they've always got back together. I know B gives him a hard time, but they're really soppy about each other. I can hardly say the same for me and Grant, can I?

25 April 1997

What did I say about motherhood being easy? Whatever I said, forget it. Courtney's waking up every two or three hours at night, and I've got bags under me eyes that I could put shopping in. Trying to figure out why she's crying is the main problem. Is she hungry, tired, overtired, dirty, bored, in pain, frightened…? You just wish they could tell yer. Tony's not being quite so understanding now he's got to get up in the mornings, and with him and Simon out all day I'm going mad here on me own. The place is a complete tip, I seem to live in me dressing-gown, and I would kill for even four hours straight, uninterrupted sleep.

That racket from upstairs ain't helping any. I can practically see the ceiling vibrating when Joe turns his music up loud. You'd think Lorraine would make him show a bit of consideration with a little baby downstairs. Did I say they moved into the top flat? I can't shake the woman off! I can even hear it when Grant's up there. It's torture. I mean, I don't actually hear them doing it, but it's in my head, I imagine it. Especially when I see him leave in the morning and he's got that smug look on his face. Anyways, it won't be long now before we get the test results. And once Grant knows we're his family, her upstairs can sling her hook.

28 April 1997

Well, Courtney, guess who your daddy is? I was right all along. It's Grant! I must admit, when the letters came through the door – one for me and one for Tony – I was dead nervous. Tony just froze, then he said, 'Day of reckoning, eh?' He tore his open. I couldn't look at mine, I just watched his face. He was trying to look like he was OK, but I knew he weren't. He said, 'Well, you got what you wanted, Tiff. She's Grant's.' Then he added, 'poor kid,' and stomped off to the bathroom. I tried not to show how happy I was, but I wanted to run round the flat shouting, 'Yes, yes, yes!'

I thought Grant might come round straight off, but he didn't. I couldn't sit still indoors, so I took her out to the clinic to get weighed. Saw B in the market and told her the good news. She wasn't exactly over the moon, but then she's never been Grant's number one fan. At least I got to tell Lorraine first. Put her nose severely out of joint. She went rushing off, and not long after, the proud father himself showed up on my doorstep. He came in and picked Courtney up and cuddled her, then he said, 'I never noticed it before, but she's got my nose.' He was really swept away. I told him, 'We owe it to her to both be there for her,' and he said, 'I'll be there for her, you can count on it,' and my heart did a sort of flip. Then he went, 'Look, Tiff, don't hold your breath, nothing's changed between us,' and I went down like a pricked balloon. But I'm not gonna give up yet. There's still plenty of time.

1 May 1997

Another visit from Grant today. I could tell by the tone of his voice he weren't there for a friendly chat. He was getting all heavy-handed about having access to Courtney and was really taken aback when I simply goes, 'Fine, yeah, you should see her. Come over any time you want.' I think he was expecting a big fight.

There was a bit of a to-do upstairs this evening. Joe went berserk and held Lorraine prisoner in the flat and they had to get the police and an ambulance and a social worker and a psychiatrist before he would come out. He's been sectioned, apparently. Lorraine really lost it afterwards and started ranting at everybody cos there was this big crowd outside. God, if I'd known what kind of nutter I had living above me, I don't know what I'd have done. I mean, what about Courtney's safety?

On the other hand, I can't help feeling a bit sorry for Lorraine, even though I hate her guts. I know I ain't been a mum long, but it's long enough to know that if it's your own child in trouble, you'll do anything to protect them. Anything. The love I feel for Courtney is so strong, it's like nothing I've ever felt before, even for a bloke. It's a really primitive feeling, like you'd die for them if it was necessary. Scary.

12 May 1997

It's really hard to keep this diary going cos I'm too knackered to write it half the time. I don't know whether I'm coming or going. The other day I was so done in after being up half the night that Simon took Courtney to work in the baby sling while I caught up on some shut-eye. Sanjay's customers thought she was really cute. Perhaps I'm onto a winner there – although Simon says Grant went past and gave him a dirty look, so it obviously didn't go down too well with him.

Grant had a right go at me today for taking Courtney into the Vic. He said it was too smoky for her, which I admit it is, but Simon had offered to buy me a drink and it's not as if I get to go out much these days. Anyways, I thought it was best not to cause a scene, so I left, and it must have worked cos later Grant came round and offered to babysit so as I could go to Lenny's birthday party. I could hardly believe him at first when he came out with it. I said, 'Have you had a bang on the head or something?' and he went, 'Like you said, you need a break.'

Well! I didn't need asking twice. I've been dying to get me gladrags on again – I've lost a bit of weight and me figure's beginning to look almost acceptable. Do you know how long it's been since I've had a dance? I got there and said to them all, 'I've come to show you how it's done.' Lenny's eyes were on stalks! B was on a bit of a downer. Turns out Joe's got schizophrenia, which is pretty serious, and she's worried in case it runs in the family, he being her half-brother. I guess that's why she was so suspicious of Grant. She kept going, 'Why's he being so nice to you all of a sudden?' But I said to her, 'Maybe he's beginning to realise what a mistake he's made.' After all, there's only one way he's going to be able to get Courtney permanently. And that's by taking me back.

19 May 1997

Got another house call today – from Lorraine this time. I dunno why she came. I mean, she knows what I think about her. I told her straight, what Grant and I had was so much better than what she's got with him. She looks dead miserable all the time and they're always rowing. I can hear them upstairs. She said it'd been hard for her lately. What does she think it's been like for me, coping on my tod? I just snorted and said, 'My heart bleeds for you. Of course, when I was with Grant I was never miserable, it was the happiest time of my life.' And just in case she missed the point, I added, 'I still think about him every single day. I'll always love him. He's my every-thing.' She looked really surprised then, like it hadn't occurred to her that I might have feelings about him. That gave her something to think about.

20 May 1997

I don't know what to do. Grant says he's gonna get Courtney off me, for good. Take my baby away! I couldn't live without her, he knows that. I'm so upset, I can hardly think straight. I don't know why he's being like this. I mean, I ain't done nothing wrong. Courtney gets treated like a little princess. She gets everything she needs, no matter how skint I am, and now that he's paying maintenance she gets all the little luxuries I could never afford. She's cared for and loved and she's hardly ever out of my sight. Apart from this evening, when I went out to a wine bar with B. It's only my third night out since I had her, so I don't think that's too much to ask, and besides, it was B's idea, not mine. In fact, I got fed up after one bottle and said I wanted to go home because I was missing Courtney. When we got back to the flat, Simon was tearing his hair out and said Grant had barged in and taken her because he'd seen the gas van outside. I was furious with Simon, which wasn't fair really because I know what Grant's like when he wants something. If you stand in his way, you just get trampled on.

So I goes charging round to the Vic, with Simon and Tony – who's turned up at long flamin' last – and Grant stands in the doorway shouting, 'What sort of mother are you, leaving your baby in a death trap like that?' Simon swore that the gas man said the boiler weren't dangerous. Then Peggy comes up and goes, 'Right, Grant, let Courtney go home, she should be in bed.' Even then I could see he didn't want to hand her over, but he always listens to his mum. I tried to make it easier for him by saying I knew he was only worried about Courtney's safety, and that's when he turned on me. He was really vicious. I'm still shaking. And you know the stupid thing? Tonight I'd decided to tell him how much I love him. He didn't even let me finish my sentence.

22 May 1997

I don't think I got a wink of sleep last night. Course, it had to be the one night Courtney practically slept through. She didn't seem bothered by all the goings-on, which is more than I can say for me. I just can't see an end to all of this. It's really getting me down. Simon told B what Grant had done and she came straight round. She said Grant was a macho pig and had no right to go round stealing babies in the middle of the night and then calling me an unfit mother. I know she's right, but I don't like hearing her talk about Grant like that.

We've got no hot water and I couldn't wash me hair or bath Courtney, so B let me use their bathroom. Felt a bit better once I'd sorted us both out a bit. Simon had made arrangements for us to use Lenny's bathroom. I said thanks but no thanks. Their place is a dump! Luckily, it wasn't cold today, but I've got a fan heater now in case it gets chilly later. Grant brought it round this afternoon. He said he'd 'overreacted' yesterday, which is as much of an apology as I was likely to get from him. He was playing with Courtney and I heard him say, 'Me and your mum're not going to argue any more,' and I thought for a second he'd changed his mind and wanted me back. I mean, it's obvious him and Lorraine are on the rocks. Then he said, 'You're gonna be a very special little girl with two of every-thing. One at your mum's place and one at home with me.' It was the last straw. I said, 'You don't know what it's like for me. Every time I look at Courtney, all I see is you.' I told him I couldn't switch me feelings about him off just like that, and he said, 'Well, what do you want me to do?' and I went – this is pathetic, right, but it just all came tumbling out – 'I want you to love me, Grant. Doesn't have to be as much as I love you. Just a bit. That's all.' He didn't know what to say to that and he left really quickly. I spent the rest of the day going hot and cold whenever I thought about what a prat I'd made of meself.

26 May 1997

Peggy's being so brilliant. She's totally on my side. I took Courtney round to the Vic to see if I could bath her there because the boiler's still not back on (and it looks like we could

35

be in for quite a wait with Simon's penny-pinching landlord dragging his feet). She was delighted to see her granddaughter and when she heard what a struggle I was having without hot water, traipsing across the Square to B's with bags of towels and shampoo, she said I was welcome to come over to the Vic any time. Then she goes, 'Come to think of it, why don't you move back here until the boiler's fixed?' and shoots me this knowing look. I told her I didn't think Grant would approve, but she said, 'He can't argue with what's best for Courtney, can he?' and I had to agree there. She went on about how good it would be for him to get involved in looking after Courtney – you know, all the practical stuff, getting his hands dirty – then she said, 'I don't care what the politically correct view is, I think children should be brought up by two parents who are married to each other.' Then I realised what her game was!

So now I'm back at the Vic in the spare room. It feels really weird, because it's not my home and yet it is. Grant was pretty cheesed off when he found out, and kept going on about it only being temporary. He was even more cross because Peggy's given me my old job back behind the bar while I'm here. She pointed out to him they're short-staffed because Lorraine's going off to Bolton to look for Joe (he was discharged from the mental hospital and did a runner), so Grant didn't have a leg to stand on.

29 May 1997

I think the plan might be working. Grant's being great with Courtney, changing nappies, everything. He even came to the clinic with me this morning for Courtney's jabs. When we got back, he asked me for a photo of her to keep in his wallet. I dug out the ones they did at the hospital, but she's changed so much since then. I said we'd have to get some more done soon, and he agreed. Later on, I suggested that he took Courtney out for a walk, and he took her round to Nigel's at the video shop.

I watched him go, pushing the pram as proud as punch. He loves her to bits.

Peggy told me later that Grant's gonna drop his application for the residency order. She said he had actually admitted to her that I was a good mother and that he couldn't split me and Courtney up. I'm so relieved. And it's gotta be a good sign, ain't it? I mean, I know how much he wants to keep Courtney at the Vic, and if he's not gonna try and take her off me, there's only one other solution…

Lorraine got back today. Seemed very surprised to see me behind the bar. I didn't say anything, just gave her a look that told her, 'You're on marked time, gal.'

2 June 1997

Lorraine ain't been in to work since she got back with Joe, and Peggy can't get her on the phone, neither. Grant's in a foul mood. I reckon something's happened between them. Fingers crossed!

3 June 1997

Me and Grant was up half the night with Courtney. She had a temperature and we had to keep sponging her with lukewarm water – which she hated, poor little thing – to bring it down. She seems much better this morning, but we're both knackered. Still, it felt really good to be doing it together. It was like we was proper parents. I said so to Grant at breakfast, but he went, 'Don't start, Tiff. It ain't gonna happen. You two are going home as soon as that boiler's fixed.' I was hoping he might've come round a bit by now, but obviously it ain't working.

Peggy saw I was a bit down and had a word after Grant had gone. She said, 'He'll see sense, it's just gonna take a bit of time,' and when I pointed out I didn't exactly have time on my side, she said, 'As long as you're here in the Vic, you're in with a fighting chance,' which made me feel a bit better. She's offered to organise Courtney's christening, which I thought was a really good idea. I mean, I want Courtney to be christened anyway, and taking all those vows about our child – well, it's a really bonding thing to do, ain't it?

9 June 1997

Lorraine came back to the Vic today. I didn't think I'd be able to stand working with her, and was just about to give up on the whole idea of getting Grant back when Peggy let me into a secret – Lorraine and Grant have split up!!!

We went to see Alex, the vicar, about the christening service today. I've asked Bianca to be godmother and Simon to be godfather, though Grant ain't too happy about it. I thought I'd better keep him sweet, so I said Phil could be a godfather as well and that seemed to satisfy him.

12 June 1997

The boiler's been replaced. I haven't told Grant. I know he'll go ballistic if he finds out, but it's a risk I've got to take. Lorraine is hardly speaking to him and it's clear as day she ain't interested any more, so the field's open for me, innit?

13 June 1997

This is the day you was christened, Courtney. It was a really lovely ceremony and you were so good – didn't seem to mind getting your head wet at all. I put you in a proper little christening robe and you looked such a little cherub! Peggy was going to Alex, 'I bet you ain't had one as pretty as this in a while,' and then she went on about how Courtney was the spitting image of her as a baby (poor love, you ain't, I promise!). Alex didn't know where to put himself. Actually, he's a really nice bloke. I could almost fancy him meself if he weren't a vicar. The words he said was so passionate! He said to be a parent is the most important commitment one human can make to another. I can't remember how he put it exactly, but the gist of it was that it takes love to make a baby and it's love that helps it to grow. 'Love binds parent to parent and parent to child.' I remember that bit cos I glanced over at Grant and then Alex went on, 'It is love that creates a family and it is love that holds it together,' and Grant caught my eye and my tummy did a little flip.

It was a special moment for both of us when Alex baptised you and said your full name, Courtney Dawn Mitchell. He gave the godparents candles to hold, to show you had passed from darkness to light, and Grant looked at me again and his eyes were all shiny. Afterwards, we had our photos taken out-side, and Grant smiled at me for the first time since – well, since it all went wrong. I was so pleased, I leaned over and kissed him, and that's when Nigel took the photo. Just like Charles and Di on the balcony!

Grant was in a really good mood until we got back to the Vic. Then I saw him talking to Lorraine behind the bar and they seemed to be having a row. When Grant came back over he was all snappy and short with me again, and it was like nothing had changed. It made me feel so depressed because today, in the church, I knew that if Lorraine was out of the pic-ture, me and Grant could make it work. In the end I went over to her and said I knew she and Grant had split up and asked her what was going on. She was playing dumb, going, 'What do you mean?' So I spelled it out for her. I said, 'You hanging around here is making things difficult for me and Grant. We could have a future together but every time he sees you the whole thing goes straight out of his head.' She sort of clenched her teeth and said, 'It's nothing to do with me any more,' and so I goes, 'Then what are you still doing here? Just go away and give us a chance.' And guess what? Half an hour later, she comes over and says, 'I just quit. He's all yours, Tiffany.' Result!

Well, Courtney, me and you's back with Daddy again. Now we can be a real family, all together under one roof. It'll work out this time, I know it will.

It all happened yesterday. At first I thought we was gonna have to leave because Tony had let slip to Grant about the boiler being fixed. I tried to cover my back by saying he hadn't said nothing to me, but Grant could see I was lying and went spare. In the end, I confessed I was hoping he might get used to us being around and want us to stay, and he said it was never gonna happen and nothing had changed. So I says, 'Well, what about you and Lorraine splitting up?' and he was cross that I knew and said they was just giving each other some space and that when Joe was better things would get back to normal. I goes, 'Normal? That means getting shot of me and Courtney does it?' and he looked a bit guilty, but at that point Joe came bursting in and starts ranting and raving at us. He was well out of order, calling me a tart and shouting his head off, which of course woke Courtney up and made her cry. She was bawling for ages and by the time I got her calmed down, Joe and Grant had gone. Even then she wouldn't settle and it took me nearly half an hour before I could get her off again.

I heard Grant come back in not long after and soon as I saw him I could tell something had happened. He was all subdued and his shoulders were sort of stooped and when I asked where he'd been, he said, 'I don't want to talk about it,' and went off to his bedroom. I followed him in, partly because I wanted to get something off me chest, and partly because – well, I could see he was hurting. I told him I was really sorry for lying to him and that I should have known better and he said, 'Look, it don't matter now. Nothing matters any more,' like it was the end of the world or something. I guessed it was about Lorraine, and he said things was over between them. I've never seen him so low. He said, 'It's all my fault, I ruin everything. The closer

I get to people, the more I hurt them.' I told him it wasn't all his fault, it was just that Lorraine was the wrong person for him, but he went, 'No, no it's my fault. Look at what I've done to you.' I said it didn't matter, that I didn't care about that any more because I loved him, and he said, 'How can you say that?' I said, 'I just do. I've seen all your sides before, all your bad ones, and I don't care.' And then I kissed him. I hadn't planned it or nothing, I just did it because it felt right. He tried to stop himself, but he couldn't. He needed me so badly and I needed him. It was like we were drowning in each other's arms and we clung on to each other so tight...

Well, I'd better stop there cos you're not old enough for sex scenes yet, sweetheart. All I'll say is that we made love and it was very very special, for me anyway. Only afterwards, he gets this anxious look on his face and says, 'We shouldn't have done that. It was a mistake. I still love Lorraine.' I thought, I ain't letting you go, not now, so I goes, 'Forget her. Your future is with me and Courtney, not Lorraine. I love you. No one else is gonna love you like I do. No one.' He said he couldn't love me the way I wanted him to and if we was to get back together we could end up hurting each other more than we've ever done before. I thought, I'm gonna lose him...but then you saved the day, Courtney, by waking up and crying. I went to comfort you and while I was by your cot, I thought, I know, I'll bring her in with us because I knew he'd absolutely love that. I suppose you could say you were my trump card. My ace of hearts! He held you and whispered, 'Hello, my little princess,' and you snuggled down on his chest so trusting and I knew he was sold. I said, 'Grant it's gonna be OK, I just know it,' and we all slept together that night as a family for the first time in your life.

23 June 1997

Me and Grant are walking on eggshells, but we seem to be getting on OK. I see him looking at Lorraine sometimes though, and I know what's going through his head. It's gonna take a while before he forgets about her, especially while she's still living next door. I wish she would do the decent thing and clear off out of Walford. She came in for a drink the other day. The moment she walked through the door, I made a point of letting her see that me and Grant was back together. I took hold of his arm, looked up into his eyes and said, 'Your turn to check on Courtney, sweetheart.' When he'd gone upstairs, I turned round and said to her, 'For your information, Grant's decided he wants his marriage to work, so there's nothing to keep you here now, is there?' You could have knocked me down with a feather when she went, 'I'm really pleased for you both, Tiffany. I hope it all works out this time.' And she looked as if she meant it, too.

I'm really worried about Simon and Tony at the moment. They're being picked on by these yobs who've been causing aggro in the Square. Tony's been beaten up, and today their window got broken. Simon says Tony's 'in denial' and won't talk about it because they called him a 'dirty little queer'. Everyone in the Vic was gossiping about why him and Tony was being singled out, so Simon stood up and announced they was gay. He said it weren't a big deal for them, so why should it be for anybody else? You should have seen Peggy's face. She had no idea. I think Pauline Fowler was a bit shocked, too. Tony threw a real wobbly and went off in a strop. I don't think he was too pleased at being outed like that.

26 June 1997

Nigel and Grant had their big race round the Square today. They've been training for it for weeks, poor old Nigel toddling round after Grant, all red in the face and panting. Phil opened a book on the race and everyone was betting on Grant. Peggy was really getting into it. She made Grant this huge 'high-protein' breakfast of bacon and eggs and made him wear a red silk boxer's gown which used to belong to their dad. I admit I was getting quite excited about it, too, and I thought it would be a walkover for Grant. I mean, he's pretty fit. His pecs are like iron (I just love lying in those strong arms!). And as for his thighs – ooh, don't get me going...

Anyway, Grant was well in front, but Peggy blew it by letting go of the dog, who ran over to Grant and tripped him up. Nigel being Nigel agreed to forfeit the race and Grant invited everyone back to the pub for a drink. It was a really good laugh. Seems like the first time in months that I've been able to relax and enjoy meself. I think we've turned the corner now, me and Grant.

7 July 1997

I'm trying to plan something really special for Grant's birthday, which is tomorrow, but Peggy keeps sticking her oar in. She wants to take over everything. I didn't mind for the christening, but I wish she'd back off. I mean, I'd like me and Grant to go off somewhere on our own, have a romantic evening out together. There's some fancy restaurants down by the docks, or we could even go up West, see a movie, then go on to Chinatown maybe. He likes a nice Chinese. The best thing Peggy could do is babysit for us. I tried to suggest that, but she went, 'Oh, no, we've got to have a party for him here,' and then she just went ahead and started arranging it, despite what I'd just said.

I felt really frustrated and told B, but she weren't exactly sympathetic. She goes, 'Well, that's Peggy, ain't it? You was the one who married a Mitchell. It's like that film 'Married to the Mob' – you gotta do what the family wants, or else.' I told her I wasn't gonna be dictated to by an interfering mother-in-law and she went, 'OK, so who writes the shopping lists, then?' I had to admit it was Peggy and B said that means she's the one in control. Come to think of it, she does decide all the meals.

Well, everything, really. We even have to buy pink quilted loo rolls cos that's what she likes. I think it's time I started asserting meself.

8 July 1997

Grant's birthday. He's thirty-five. I told him I've always gone for older men, but he was a bit down about being so ancient. I gave him a really nice framed photograph of me and Courtney that I got done secretly at a photographer's studio. He was dead chuffed with it. Peggy's plans for a big do got knocked on the head because I warned Grant about it and he told her he didn't want a fuss. Anyways, she wasn't up to doing much after yesterday cos she got mobbed by this gang of kids who pushed her over and stole her handbag. Grant wanted to have a go at them, but George said he knew a better way and got a mate of his in CID to put them in the cells overnight. Grant said that was a wimp's way of dealing with things, but I reckon he was hacked off cos he was dying to thump them, and because it was George who sorted it out in the end, not him.

15 July 1997

I can't believe Tony. He's up to his old tricks again, only this time I think he's cheating on Simon – with a woman! I saw him yesterday with Polly, that journalist he works with, the one who looks like a hairdresser's worst nightmare. It was really late and he was holding her hand and leading her into the flat. Simon's away, so I knew Tony had to be up to no good. I went straight round there in the morning, but they'd already gone, so I went to the 'Gazette' office to have it out with him. He came out with this long, involved story about Polly needing a shoulder to cry on, which I found hard to swallow cos she looks as tough as old boots. I don't know whether to trust him or not. He says he still loves Simon and wouldn't do anything to hurt him, but then look what he did to me.

22 July 1997

Peggy came up with this brilliant suggestion today. She said we ought to have our marriage blessed. You know, a proper church service to renew our vows. I thought it would be fantastic – I mean, it's almost like getting married again, isn't it? But I didn't go overboard cos I didn't want Grant to think I was being pushy. I always felt as if I'd missed out a bit, getting married secretly, even though at the time I pretended I didn't. Then I went to Bianca and Ricky's wedding and it was so lovely it made me wish we'd done it like that.

Anyways, it's useless daydreaming about it because Grant said it was a daft idea. If he thought anything of me, he'd know how much it would mean to me, so I guess I've got my answer. When we got back together he said he couldn't love me the way I wanted him to, and I suppose I should just accept it. But it's hard sometimes.

28 July 1997

I don't know what made Grant change his mind, but he's agreed to the blessing after all. I think Phil must've had something to do with it cos he went round the Arches yesterday to talk to Grant. But who cares why? The important thing is, he's agreed! Today we went to see Alex Healey, the vicar, to sort things out. There's problems already – Peggy wants something along the lines of the royal wedding, whereas Grant wants to keep it low-key. Alex said we could really push the boat out if we wanted, and I got quite keen, but Grant put his foot down. He was quite sweet about it though. He said to me afterwards, 'The people that matter will be there – us and the family. That's what this is supposed to be about, not how much money we spend.' We booked it for 21 August, which don't give us much time, especially since Peggy's got the bit between her teeth and invited the whole pub to a party at the Vic afterwards. At first, Grant was absolutely livid, but he didn't know what I knew –

that Peggy's got another mammogram at the hospital next week and she's scared stiff. Organising a party is her way of taking her mind off it. She told him later, and he's been fine about things since.

11 August 1997

I've started weaning Courtney. She only seems to want to eat mashed banana at the moment, though. I tried her on a different brand of baby cereal this morning but she just spat it out. I tried to kid her it tasted lovely, but really it was horrible. She cottons on quickly! It's amazing how fast she's growing. She's really strong and she definitely knows who her mummy and daddy are. Even now, she's lost that 'tiny baby' look. It won't be long before she's sitting up by herself, and then crawling, and then walking.

It's funny, sometimes I can hardly believe what I've done, having a kid. Once you stop and think about it, the responsibility is so huge it's overwhelming. What if we get it wrong? Grant's really messed up because of his relationship with his father and I'm just as bad about my dad – not to mention Mum, who just walked out and left us when I was 12. What your parents do leaves scars. Courtney's already had to put up with me and Grant screaming at each other, even though she ain't old enough to understand why. It must affect her though, I reckon. I hope, now things is settled, we can do a better job than our lot did.

Talking of which, I got a letter from Dad this morning. Maybe that's what got me thinking like this. Apparently, he's been in hospital with pancreatitis again and wants me to visit him. Well, tough. I don't want nothing to do with him, not after his last performance. And I definitely don't want him near Courtney. Who knows what he might do? It really upset me, just being reminded about him again. Grant said I should chuck the letter in the bin, so I did.

12 August 1997

Me and Bianca have been discussing going on holiday together, like we used to back in the days before Ricky and Grant. We had some wild times! 'Dancing Queen', that's what they used to call me. Don't think our men would be too thrilled with us doing that now, so we're planning a little group holiday. B said Ricky fancied Paris because his sister, Diane, lives there. That's where Grant proposed to me, so it should be really romantic. I thought we could make it a post-blessing holiday, like a second honeymoon, you know? Only thing is, I ain't told Grant yet. Well, not everything. He liked the idea of us going away somewhere on our own. I'm gonna break the news about Bianca and Ricky to him gently...

18 August 1997

I got some flowers from Dad today. Why is it that they feel like a threat, not a gift? If he thinks he can get round me with a few carnations, he's mistaken. As soon as I realised who they were from, I threw them out. Grant found them in the dustbin, so I had to tell him. I thought he would do his nut but he said if Dad turns up here, he'd deal with him. Grant's being really supportive at the moment. He didn't even mind about B and Ricky coming on holiday with us. Actually, we probably won't see that much of them cos they'll be staying with Diane and Grant's gonna book us into a swanky hotel.

There's only three days to go till the blessing and I'm beginning to panic. Peggy's gone to Spain to see Sam, and now there's an air-traffic controllers' strike and she's stuck in Malaga. How am I gonna manage if she don't get back here in time? She's the one that made all the arrangements, I don't know anything about the catering or the flowers or the party.

At least I've got my outfit. It's a really nice ivory-coloured jacket and skirt. Classy, you know? Not too tarty, but makes the best of what I've got. I'm gonna keep it quite simple, just have my hair up – I don't see meself as a hat person. Courtney's going to look her best, too. We bought her this darling little outfit with matching lacy bonnet and bloomers and she's got a little floral hoop to carry. Ahhh!

21 August 1997

I thought today was gonna be a total disaster. There was still no sign of Peggy when we got up, and the airline didn't know whether she was on the flight leaving this morning or not. Courtney wouldn't stop crying, the caterers were late, the cake shop sent me a hideous *wedding* cake with a bride and groom on top, and, to cap it all, Grant's Aunt Sal arrives as Peggy's stand-in. Fat lot of help she was. All she did was dither about, saying, 'What we need is a nice cup of tea.' I said to B what I needed was a nice stiff gin, so I made us both one to drink upstairs while we got ready. B went really pale and said the smell of it was making her feel like throwing up. I said, 'Either you're coming down with something or you're pregnant,' and then she admitted she was a bit late. Watch this space!

Then, on the way to the church, Grant drops this bombshell on me, saying he's booked us into the same hotel that him and Sharon stayed at in Paris. I mean, he didn't put it like that, he just mentioned he'd been there before, but I managed to worm the rest out of him. I couldn't believe he could be that insensitive! I told him he had to change it cos I wasn't stopping there, and he said, 'Fine, you try and find somewhere decent for four people at short notice on a bank holiday weekend.' When I reminded him Bianca and Ricky were staying with Diane, he goes, 'Yeah, I know, but Phil and Kathy are coming with us,' which was the first I knew of it. I said, 'Right, stop the car,' and we had a huge row in George Street, which made us late. We drove the rest of the way without speaking and when we got to the church, Grant said, 'Are we going in there or what?' I said yes, but only on condition that we stay somewhere else in Paris.

It got worse. Dad was waiting for me outside the church. He was completely pie-eyed and ranting about why hadn't he been invited and calling me all sorts of horrible names. It made me feel really shaky. Grant got hold of him and told him he'd break every bone in his body if he set one foot inside the church. I said, 'You stay out of my life, you're no part of it any more, I've got my own family now.' I was determined that he wasn't going to ruin my big day. Bianca was waiting for us, holding Courtney, and we went inside, me and Grant walking up the aisle hand-in-hand. Just as we got to the front, where the vicar was waiting for us, who should burst in the door but Peggy, carrying all her suitcases and wearing a straw hat!

I can't remember much about the ceremony, but it was really moving. I do remember the bit about us loving and cherishing each other till parted by death because it made me want to cry. I could tell Grant was moved, too, because he reached out and put his arm around me and gave me a little squeeze. It was so nice that we could include Courtney in the service. I held her and Alex said a prayer for us as a family, and she gurgled and smiled and loved every minute. She was a right little star.

The reception went really well too. Someone had sorted the cake and put a white rose and some ribbon on top instead of the awful figurines, and everybody was drinking champagne and having a good time. Grant was so sweet. He came over to me and gazed into my eyes and whispered, 'You look great,' which made my knees go all melty. I said, 'So, no regrets?' and he shook his head, and then I noticed he had put his wedding ring back on, which he hasn't worn since New Year. I know Grant isn't one for saying much, but he didn't need to. That said it all.

26 August 1997

Just finished packing for the holiday. I can't wait! We're only going for three nights, and Peggy's offered to look after

Courtney. I've booked us into this mega-posh place just outside Paris. It looks like a fairytale castle. Haven't got round to telling Grant how much it's gonna cost – serves him right for trying to palm me off with second-best. I don't want him mooning around thinking, 'This is where me and Sharon watched the sunset' or whatever. Like I told him at the blessing, this is a fresh start for us. It's a pity we've gotta have his alcoholic brother tagging along. I mean, I like Kathy, and Phil's OK when he's sober, but I wanted me and Grant to have this time to ourselves. I was hoping the price of the hotel might put them off from staying there, but when I showed Kathy the brochure, she loved it.

B's definitely pregnant. She ain't happy about it, but I think it's great. I said to her, 'We can be young mums together and our kids'll be able to grow up with each other,' but she don't see it that way. She ain't even told Ricky yet. She was going on about her mum being ground down by having kids and saying she weren't gonna let it happen to her. I don't think she's even sure whether she's gonna keep it. Having been in that position meself, I can sympathise, but my views on abortion have changed a lot since I had Courtney. It's not for religious reasons or nothing, it's just that I can't imagine life without my baby. If I'd had an abortion – well, I don't like to think about it because she wouldn't be with me now – I'd have missed out on bringing this wonderful little person into the world.

28 August 1997

Well, we're here! I'm sitting by the pool, working on me tan and writing this. Grant's gone upstairs to check on Kathy. Phil disappeared last night and didn't come back, so she must be feeling pretty low. They had a huge bust-up over a woman he's been seeing on the sly. (I must admit I find it hard to imagine anyone going wild over Phil, but it takes all sorts, eh?) She sent a letter in a perfumed envelope to Phil at the hotel and the receptionist gave it to him yesterday when we arrived. Course, Kathy smelt a rat straight off (a love-rat – ha!) and I was pretty suspicious, too. I made Grant tell me what was going on cos I knew Phil would've told him, and he said her name was Lorna and she's in his counselling group.

It put a damper on the holiday right away. I said, 'What is it with you men? Why can't you keep your flamin' trousers on?' I mean, affairs never make anyone happy, do they? We had a bit of an argument, and by dinner Grant was knocking back the wine like there was no tomorrow. When I told him to go steady, he said, 'I wanna make sure I sleep tonight.' Charming! Course, it riled me, and I ended up having a dig at him about Sharon just to wind him up. Works every time. I said, 'I can't understand what you both saw in her,' because it's true. I mean, she weren't that good-looking. In fact, I always thought she was rather fat.

Anyways, I thought, well, if you can't beat 'em, join 'em, and put away a few glasses of vino meself and we both ended up getting quite drunk. Things got a bit better after that and we had a little stroll in the grounds and talked about the future and Courtney growing up and us being grandparents ourselves one day, and by the time we went to bed we was on quite friendly terms, if you get my drift.

11.30pm: Just thought I'd update this now. Grant's asleep, but I can't settle. I feel so happy and buzzy inside. Me and Grant went to Chantilly this morning. I was reading in the guidebook all about it, and I said to Grant, 'Right, I'm gonna pretend to be Marie Antoinette and you've gotta be Louis the whatever he was. You're wooing me, but I'm playing hard to get, so you've got to offer me things.' He thought I was barking, but I was just trying to be romantic, you know? I said, 'Didn't you ever play kings and queens when you was a kid?' cos me and Simon did all the time. He thought that was hilarious and said, 'I won't ask who was who.'

I might have known it weren't Grant's cup of tea, but I suppose I just wanted him to make a fuss of me, show me I was special. It's difficult sometimes, feeling I'll always come second. Sharon was such a big influence on Grant's life, and then there was Lorraine… I asked him if he loved me, and he said, 'Of course,' and then I said, 'Are you happy?' and he went, 'I guess.' I tell you, getting Grant to sweet-talk a girl is like trying to get blood out of a stone! I said, 'Is that the best you can do?' and he said, 'I'm very happy with you,' so we got there in the end.

I think he was a bit worked up about Phil going off, though he said he weren't gonna get involved. He went up to see Kathy again when we got back and after that he was very quiet. I asked how she was and he said she just wanted to be left alone. Later, when we was having dinner, he started staring at me really closely and I thought I must've got spinach on me teeth or something, but he said, 'All that stuff you were asking earlier on today…I just want you to know this has been the best it's ever been for me.' I was so taken aback I almost choked. I said, 'Grant Mitchell, are you being romantic?' and he took my hand and said, 'I'm trying.' Gave me a warm glow all over! We skipped the pudding and went up to our room…

29 August 1997

We're home. A day earlier than expected, but then things didn't exactly go as planned. It's a shame cos I was having a really nice time until Phil turned up and ruined everything. Me and Grant made a deal. I agreed to go to the Bastille and in return he agreed to come shopping. I got the better deal cos all that's left of the Bastille is a line of paving stones, and so we spent the morning in boutiques. Grant spent a fortune on a couple of new dresses for me. I made sure I showed my appreciation when we got back to the hotel!

Afterwards, we went down to the bar before lunch and I was just ordering the drinks when this arm reaches over me shoulder and slams a glass down in front of me. I turned around and there was Phil. He stank like a brewery – correction, he stank, full stop. He was really red in the face and he said, 'I'll have a pastis, please.' I knew he was supposed to be on the wagon, so I went, 'I don't think that's a very good idea, Phil,' and he just laid into me. He was vile. He said, 'You're pretty but you're no Sharon and you never will be.' He went on about Grant, saying he'd never got over her and no matter what I did, he never would. I was so upset, I just ran out. I went upstairs to tell Kathy, and she was in a state, too, because her room had been done over and she suspected it was Phil, looking for cash. I brought her back downstairs to the bar and Phil started saying all this rubbish about Grant fancying her and what a disappointment she was with her kit off. Really nasty stuff. I thought Grant was gonna deck him right there.

Kathy just wanted to go home so we packed up and left Phil behind. Last thing I saw was him lying face down in the driveway. Totally pathetic he was. All the same, I was amazed Grant left him there.

3 September 1997

Phil still ain't showed yet and Peggy's doing her nut. Whatever Grant says, I know he's really worried about him too. I'm more worried about B. She still ain't told Ricky about the baby and she keeps chopping and changing her mind about what she's gonna do. She think's Ricky's gonna dump her just because of something he said about kids when they was at Diane's. I kept telling her that was nonsense, but she wouldn't listen.

In the end, I had a brainwave. I told Ricky I thought I could hear Courtney crying and asked him to come upstairs with me to help change her. Course, Courtney was fast asleep, so we just peeked at her and I started talking to him about babies. He was really into them, going on about how brilliant it must be, the first smile, first tooth, first step. I said, 'Have you ever wondered what your baby would look like?' And he admitted he had and I knew then that he'd make a fantastic father. We went back down and I told B how Ricky was, and you know what she said? 'It's too late.' She'd only gone and made an appointment at the abortion clinic, hadn't she.

8 September 1997

Dad phoned today, from the hospital. He sounded terrible – really raspy, rattling breath. He said he was on his way out and that he wanted me and Simon to come and see him so he could make his peace with us before he died. I don't know what to do. I don't think I could live with meself if he popped his clogs and I'd ignored his last wish. However much I hate him, he's still me own flesh and blood. I think I'm talking meself into it, aren't I?

Bianca's decided to keep the baby, thank goodness. The doctor at the clinic wouldn't let her go through with the abortion until she'd talked to Ricky, and of course he was over the moon when she told him. I've been telling Courtney she'll have a little playmate next year. I'm sure she understands stuff I say now cos she gave a big grin and bounced up and down!

9 September 1997

Went to see Dad. I hardly recognised him. I was looking round the ward and then this frail old boy croaked, 'Tiff, over here.' He seemed to have shrunk and his skin was kind of papery and grey and his pyjamas looked miles too big for him. I thought, that's me Dad, that's the monster I still have nightmares about? Suddenly he weren't scary at all, just old and sad and pathetic. The doctor came round while we was there and me and Simon had a chat with her. She said Dad was very sick and if he had one more attack it would probably be his last. She went on about how he was going to need lots of support from his family! I mean!! Dad had obviously told her we was gonna look after him. It's just so typical of him, trying to trick us like that. Simon was furious and wanted to go, but I felt a bit bad about leaving Dad in the lurch. Even though I totally agree with Simon that we don't owe Dad anything, I can't think who else would help him. Are we just gonna let him drink himself to death in the gutter?

Talking of which, Phil turned up today. He looked like a disgusting old tramp – filthy, smelly and his clothes was all shabby and torn. Peggy was pleased to see him, but Grant was really cold towards him. As for Kathy, she ain't come out of hiding since we got back from Paris. She says she's gonna divorce him. He's staying in the spare room here, worse luck. At least he's had the decency to apologise to me about the things he said. I told him about the state me dad's in because of booze. I let him have it, both barrels. 'Do you want Ben to grow up thinking of you like that? Cos I tell you, I got no respect for Dad and Ben won't have none for you, neither, if you carry on the way you're going.' He was really subdued and admitted their dad was a drinker, too, which Grant never told me. I said, 'Well, you should know better then, shouldn't you?'

16 September 1997

Peggy's let Dad move in here. I think he must have told her his sob story, but it's not like Peggy to be so easily taken in. Grant's really angry and thinks I had something to do with it, but I didn't. I admit I was worried about him cos he rang the other day saying he was due to be discharged soon and he had nowhere to go. He turned up here this morning, but Grant put his foot down, so I thought that was that.

He's staying in the spare room now and Phil's taken himself off to Scotland. I think Phil and Peggy must've had a row cos I caught her crying earlier and George was putting his arm around her. I tell you, it's like Clapham Junction in here with all the comings and goings and whatnot. It ain't good for

Courtney, all these new faces and disturbances to her routine. I wish the three of us could have our own place.

29 September 1997

Poor old Simon's got Tony's mum living with them. We've still got Dad here, so between us we're both lumbered. Simon says Irene's an evil, manipulative woman and she's trying to turn Tony against him. Dad, on the other hand, is trying so hard to be nice, it's painful to watch. He's being all smarmy with Peggy (a little flattery goes a long way with her) and keeps offering to help out in the bar. He even tried to clean the windows! It's driving Grant up the wall, and of course muggins here is getting the backlash. At least Dad's being pleasant to me, which makes a change. Wonder how long he'll manage to keep it up?

We ain't the only ones having to put up family. Diane and her son, Jacques, turned up out the blue on Bianca and Ricky's doorstep three weeks ago and they're still here. B's going potty – she says the flat's a mess and Diane lolls around like Lady Muck and don't lift a finger to help. I told her it's that bohemian lifestyle Diane's used to in Paris – which is obviously an artistic excuse for not doing the washing up.

2 October 1997

Grant caught Dad stealing drinks behind the bar and secretly topping up his hip flask from the optics. I knew his little act wouldn't last. I gave him a right rollicking and told him if Grant flung him out on his ear he needn't come to me for help. Later I spotted him and Irene flirting (least, I think that's what she was doing – hard to tell with her face). It was like watching tortoises mating on one of them nature programmes – repulsive but fascinating. I suppose you have to give 'em marks for trying at their age.

9 October 1997

God, I can't believe this. Bianca's little brother Billy has been kidnapped. He's the key witness to a bank robbery and they've taken him hostage. The Jacksons have got the police camped outside their house and Carol has just made an appeal on telly. She's being so brave. I sat and watched it with tears streaming down my face. I just don't know what I'd do if anybody snatched Courtney. I think I'd kill 'em with me bare hands. B's in a real state about it, poor girl. She's round there now, keeping Carol and Alan and the kids company.

14 October 1997

Billy's been found, safe and well. Gita came in and told us the news and everyone went running out the Vic and waited outside number 25 for him to return. The press turned up too and there was quite a party. The bad news is, Billy's still got to give evidence in court. B says it's deadly serious and the police are worried the cons might try something else. They're talking about relocating the whole family for their own safety. I'd be terrified if it were me. B's so worried, she don't know what to do.

16 October 1997

The Jacksons left the Square today. B's really cut up about it. She was crying her eyes out when they drove off. Apparently, the kidnappers had taken pictures of Billy, Sonia and Robbie cos they sent them to Carol as a warning. There weren't any pics of B, so the police think she'll be OK, and she's got a different surname now, so they ain't likely to make the connection. I told her I'd always be there for her, anytime she wanted to talk. I know how vulnerable she must be feeling, being pregnant an' all.

23 October 1997

I got back from doing some shopping this morning to find that Dad had moved out. Simon's hopping mad because Irene's offered him their sofa. Peggy said it was his own doing and that he didn't want to 'outstay his welcome', but I bet Grant and Phil had something to do with it. Phil got back a few days ago and I've seen the two of them with their heads together. I shoulda guessed what they was plotting. Short of a crowbar, I can't think of any other way of getting rid of Dad. Come to think of it, that's probably what they used.

3 November 1997

It's our wedding anniversary in a couple of weeks. I can't believe what we've been through in a year – it feels like about ten years to me! Grant hadn't mentioned anything about it, so I thought I'd better jog his memory, just in case. I mean, it would be nice to go away for a weekend or something, specially seeing as our last holiday was such a disaster. I went to the travel agents in the high street and got them to post Grant a brochure, hoping he'd take the hint. Guess what he did? Chucked it in the bin without even looking at it. Suppose I shouldn't get me hopes up. I'm an old married lady with a kid, ain't I? Romance has gone out the window these days. I'm beginning to feel as if Tiffany don't exist no more. I'm a mother, a wife, a barmaid, a daughter-in-law... If I walk down the road without the pram, I feel as if I've got a limb missing. I love Courtney and I love Grant, but it would be good to have a bit of me back. I'm only 21. I've got my whole life ahead of me still. I ain't gonna fade into the furniture, not now, not ever!

10 November 1997

Grant and Phil have gone off to Italy to help Ian Beale track down Cindy and the kids. I said I didn't mind him going, so long as he kept away from the senoritas or whatever they're called over there. I think Phil's only doing it to try and get back in Kathy's good books, which anybody can see is a waste of time. She don't wanna have nothing to do with him.

I'm right cheesed off with him too because he's kicking B and Ricky out of their flat and moving back in himself. I mean, I know it's his flat, but B's pregnant, she don't need any more stress after what she's just been through. She's staying at her mum's at the moment, so she don't even know what's going on. It's probably just as well cos Diane's done a runner and dumped Jacques on them while she goes on tour with her musician boyfriend. Poor old Ricky's tearing his hair out.

There's one piece of good news, though – Lorraine's finally leaving Walford. She's got back together with her ex-boyfriend, Peter, and she's got a new job up in Bolton. I don't mean to sound catty, but I'll be glad to see her go. I still feel twitchy whenever Grant talks to her. Lorraine and Peter was in the bar the other night and I could tell Grant was jealous. I just want that chapter of me life over, you know?

13 November 1997

Grant came into the Vic looking all suntanned and sexy and swept me off my feet. He went, 'Chow bellissima!' and I said, 'Chow yourself,' cos that's what they say in Italy. Turns out they got Ian's kids back by snatching them from their childminder. Peggy was thrilled to bits, but I couldn't help feeling for Cindy. I mean, imagine coming home and finding your children have been taken away – to another country – and there was nothing you could do about it. I know she took 'em off Ian, but even so. She's their mother. Suppose it made me remember the time Grant was trying to get Courtney off me. It still makes me shudder to think how different things might've been. I said so to Grant and he got up and kissed me and said, 'You are a very different person from Cindy. Besides, that was before I knew you,' which made me feel better.

Everyone was going to Nigel's party later on, to see Lorraine and Joe off. I didn't feel like going – for obvious reasons – so I told Grant it was probably best if he said goodbye to her on his own. He gave me a hug and went, 'What I want to do tonight is relax and spend an evening with the mother of my kid. Without the kid actually being there.' Romantic, eh? Take back what I've said before! I'll have to send him to Italy more often!

I must admit, I felt a bit worried going in, with everyone making a fuss of Lorraine. I stayed well clear of her and I was having quite a nice time, till I saw her go over to Grant. She was laughing and she reached out and touched his face – you know, the sort of thing you do when you've been close to someone? Really familiar, yeah? I felt this icy cold shiver run down my spine and I just turned and walked out the room and went to get my coat. Grant must've seen cos he followed me and asked what the matter was. I said, 'Nothing,' cos I didn't want a scene, but he went, 'No, something's wrong, come here,' and sat me down on the bed. He explained Lorraine had been teasing him cos he'd been playing this daft party game, drinking beer standing on his head. Then he said, 'Lorraine's the past now. It's me and you that's got a future. I've got a wife, a daughter and a wedding anniversary coming up. That's worth one hell of a lot to me.'

I was so pleased cos I thought he'd forgotten all about it, and he went, 'Oh right, do I look like the sort of man who wants to be hit over the head with a shovel?' I goes, 'I would've an' all,' and we had a laugh about it. After that, I really enjoyed meself and I even wished Lorraine good luck!

20 November 1997

We had a lovely anniversary yesterday – eventually. Peggy had organised another big bash to celebrate it (what is it with that woman and parties?), which wasn't what we wanted at all. I mean, your first wedding anniversary's special, innit? You want it to be intimate, just you and your husband, not have all your neighbours breathing down your neck. I don't want me memories to be of Dot Cotton getting tiddly on the sherry, do I? Grant was pretty hacked off with Peggy – he told her she'd turned it into a circus – because he'd already arranged something for the two of us. In the end, he didn't tell Peggy that we weren't going to be there and simply whisked me away to this really swish restaurant up West. It's just as well I was wearing one of them new frocks he got me in Paris! I felt a bit guilty about us leaving Peggy in the lurch, but Grant said maybe it would teach her not to interfere in future. I said, 'I doubt it,' cos that's her favourite hobby!

24 November 1997

I've got chickenpox. The doc says I've just gotta stay in bed until it gets better. It's really catching, so I ain't allowed to have Courtney near me. Grant's looking after her – he's got her strapped in the baby sling while he's working. Neither of us likes having her down in the smoky bar, but we ain't got no choice. I feel like I'm in quarantine. Peggy comes in with a hanky over her face, like I've got the plague or something, even though she's already had it. I'm covered in this revolting rash and I look disgusting. Feel too awful to write any more.

16 December 1997

I can't believe how long I've had this soddin' illness. It completely floored me for a while. I'm still really groggy and if I get up, my head goes all swimmy. My hair's like rats' tails cos it ain't been washed and me legs have gone like skinny little sticks. They're so weak I can only just get to the bathroom and back. Today I managed as far as the kitchen, then wished I hadn't. I got to the door, which was open slightly, and I heard Peggy going on to Grant about how George wanted her to move in with him. Then she said, 'I told him it was impossible anyway because you and Tiffany will need me around when you've got number two. You think you can cope now, but wait till Courtney's toddling and you've got another little one to look after.' I was so gobsmacked I just went back to bed.

To be honest, the thought of having another kid ain't crossed my mind. Well, you know, one day perhaps, but I've got a lot of living to do first. Me and Grant ain't even discussed it, so what's he said to Peggy? That's what I want to know. It's so typical of him. If he wants something, he just assumes I want it, too. I mean, I reckon I've got a pretty important part to play in making another baby!

18 December 1997

Dr Legg came to see me today and says I'm over the worst now and that I can have visitors. I said, 'Does that mean I can see Courtney?' and he said yes. But after he left, Peggy started going on about how she shouldn't be exposed to any risk, so Grant's still keeping her away from me. I miss her so much! I'm worried that she'll have forgotten who her mummy is. It's been almost a month now, poor lamb.

Bianca came round later and I started telling her how much I missed Courtney. As soon as the words was out of my mouth I felt absolutely terrible. Bianca had to abort her baby because the scan showed it had spina bifida. She was looking so washed out and there I was going on about how I hadn't seen my baby for a few weeks and she'd just lost hers for ever. I said, 'B, I'm so sorry,' but she said, 'No, it's OK, Tiff, I'm alright.' She was being so strong about it, and they'd only had the baby's funeral three days ago. Frank paid for it. B called the baby Natasha, which is a beautiful name, I think. It's so sad. They moved into Lorraine's old flat and last thing I saw, Ricky was turning Joe's old room into this gorgeous nursery, putting little bunny stencils on the wall and buying a cot and everything. I dunno how B can bear it, sleeping next door. It must be hell.

22 December 1997

I'm up and about again, thank goodness. It's still like Clapham Junction in here – that interfering old cow Aunt Sal's in the spare room now (trouble with Uncle Harold – and who can blame him?). She's always trying to tell me what to do with Courtney. I could brain her sometimes. I've been feeling really wound up all day, ever since Peggy told me that she weren't gonna marry George after all because, 'What would you two do without me?' I can think of a few things, straight off. Rearrange the furniture, have me friends up, get rid of her knick-knacks, cook what I like for tea, have sex on the sofa... Grant's really laid back about it, which makes me cross, too. He's a big boy now, it's time he cut those apron strings.

I suppose that was why I had a go at him earlier. I was trying to be romantic and he came on all strong, but instead of getting turned on I just felt really angry? I pushed him away and of course he gets cross and accuses me of playing games with him. I said, 'Alright, I'll tell you what's the matter. There's sex and there's love. I know the difference, even if you don't.' Then I chucked him out the bedroom and he had to sleep on the sofa.

24 December 1997

Me and Grant still ain't speaking. It's been an awful day today. It started bad, with Phil telling us Roy Evans had a heart attack in the Square last night, and it's got worse as the day went on. Aunt Sal was being her usual nosy self and winding me up something chronic. She took Courtney off for a walk in her pushchair and left her outside the café, completely unattended. B found her there crying and wheeled her up the road, so when Sal comes out, she thinks Courtney's been stolen. Grant was trying to blame B, but I said thank goodness Bianca did take her. I mean, who knows what pervert could've come along? Sal should never have left her by herself. I'm breaking out in a sweat now, just thinking about it.

Peggy rounded up everybody for Midnight Mass this evening. We all went, except for Simon, who's stopping at the Vic because him and Tony have broken up. B was at the service, looking very down, so I invited her and Ricky and Frank over for Christmas lunch tomorrow. Course, this caused a row because I never checked with Peggy first, then Grant weighed in and said I should consult with him before I do anything. (I mean! What century does he think we live in?) I says, 'I'm your wife, you should back me up,' and he goes, 'Then start acting like it.' He made me so mad I chucked him out the bedroom again. Next thing I see, Grant out in the Square with his arms around these two tarts who was in the bar earlier. He saw me looking and just stared up at me. I dunno whether to go downstairs or not. I'm scared of what I might find…

25 December 1997

It's Christmas Day night and I can't sleep. Grant's gone off somewhere. I don't know where – Phil's probably. Suddenly, my life's falling to pieces. I can't work out why it's gone so wrong so quickly. I mean, before I was ill, we were getting on really well. Now all Grant seems to want me for is having another baby. If we have sex, it's just to try and get me pregnant. Well, that's what it seems like to me. No wonder I ain't interested. I think he sees me as some sort of kiddie production line, not a person at all. Hey, I've written all this before, haven't I? This is really depressing.

Then there was those girls. Grant said he didn't do nothing, even though they wanted some kinda kinky threesome with him. Apparently, he brought them back to the Vic to 'prove a point'. Or did he mean teach me a lesson? Cos that's how it felt. He made me go to bed with him afterwards and I felt totally humiliated.

I was determined to put it behind me and have some fun today, but he's been niggling at me for any little thing – kissing

Frank under the mistletoe, babysitting Ben while Kathy goes to the refuge, having a giggle with Conor in the bar. Conor's this Irish guy with wild curly hair and a lovely lilting voice. He's a big flirt, but then I am, too, and I have to say it was really nice to have someone pay me a few compliments after the way Grant's been treating me. Conor said how lovely I was looking and that if I wasn't a married woman we could have some serious fun. I says, 'If I wasn't a married woman, then I'd probably be all for it,' because Grant was winding me up so much. He heard (well, he was meant to) and he went storming out the Vic. He didn't come back, and later I saw him drinking under the Christmas tree in the middle of the Square. It's 3.00am and there's still no sign of him. Happy Christmas, Tiff.

27 December 1997

I dunno where to begin. I think I might in shock, actually. The past 48 hours don't seem real at all. I mean, I'm back here, at the Vic, but there was a time last night when I was beginning to think I wouldn't get out of my room alive. Grant just went mad. Really crazy, out-of-control violence. It was terrifying. I've seen him angry before, loads of times, but I've never seen him like that.

It was all because I was having a good time and enjoying meself. Grant totally overreacted. Peggy had organised this Boxing Day party in the Vic, with games and forfeits and all, and Bianca's forfeit was to dance an Irish jig. She was making a right pig's ear of it, so Conor got up and joined in, and he pulled me up too, and we were having a laugh. I tried to get Grant to come and dance with us and he just turned his back on me. I could tell he weren't happy. He'd been in a bad mood all day cos he had a hangover from the bottle of whisky he drank at Phil's on Christmas night.

Anyway, Sal said Courtney was crying, so I went through to the hall to have a listen and Grant follows me. He says, 'What are you trying to do?' and I says, 'Have a good time, that's all,' and he goes, 'Are you trying to make a fool of me?' So I says no, and I'm about to go up and see to Courtney when he says, 'Where are you going? I'm talking to you,' in that nasty voice he uses sometimes. I was so cross, I went, 'Yeah, but I've heard it all before Grant and it's boring me. Come to think of it, maybe that's why I don't sleep with you, cos you're boring in bed as well' – which is true. I mean, he don't go out of his way to please me or nothing.

It was stupid of me to taunt him like that, I know, but I didn't expect him to lose it like he did. He came chasing after me with this twisted expression on his face and I said, 'Don't you touch me,' and he shouted, 'Touch you? I'm gonna kill you. I should've sorted you out a long time ago.' I bolted up the stairs and locked meself in the bedroom and my heart was thumping like a drum. He was trying to knock the door down and calling me a slag and I was screaming, but no one could hear us because they were all doing the hokey-cokey down-stairs. Then this fist came smashing through the door, like in 'The Shining', and Grant burst in and backed me into a corner. Well, I was dead scared, but I stood up to him and we had this blazing row, then he said – this is really hard for me to write – he said, 'I don't love you, I never have. You're just a second-rate scrubber who happened to have my baby. If it weren't for Courtney I'd have dumped you ages ago.' I said, 'I don't believe you,' and he said, 'It's true. You disgust me. Sometimes I can hardly bear to even look at you.' He was right in my face and shouting. I tried to block my ears but he took my hands away and said, 'When we make love, I ain't thinking of you. In my head I'm always with Sharon.' I was so upset, I tried to get past him, but he wouldn't move so I slapped him. He got hold of my wrists, then he pushed me away suddenly, really hard. I fell backwards and hit my head on the bedside table. It hurt so much I thought I was gonna faint. You know what? He didn't even help me. He stood over me, going, 'Have you had enough, now? You're nothing to me, Tiffany, nothing.' And then he just walked out and left me lying there.

It was Phil who came to look for me. I was in the kitchen, trying to stop the bleeding, and he found me and bathed the cut on my head. He asked me not to give up on Grant, but I told him Grant had crossed the line and there was no going back. I got Courtney all bundled up in a blanket and I took her over to Bianca and Ricky's. B said I should leave Grant and I knew she was right, but then Grant came round later and he wanted to apologise and I didn't know which one of them to listen to. Me head said Bianca and me heart said Grant. In the end, I knew I had to hear him out, though B tried to stop me.

Grant said he didn't mean all the stuff he'd said, that he'd just wanted to hurt me and it wasn't true about Sharon. I told him I didn't believe him and that I was gonna leave. That really shook him. He could see I was serious. I suppose we'd both calmed down a bit by then cos we started talking about our marriage. I said I didn't want to be stuck changing nappies all me life and that I wanted to get out and live a little, get a different job, maybe go back to college. I told him, 'You got me pinned to the spot like I'm some kinda insect and if you don't like what's going on, you hit out.' It just reminded me so much of my dad, seeing Grant standing over me with that look of hate on his face. I said, 'I can't live like that, not knowing when you're gonna lash out, always being afraid of you.'

And then it all came out. How he gets jealous and he can't hack it, not after what Sharon and Phil did to him. That's why he panicked when he saw me with Conor – he thought I didn't need him any more. He said, 'From now on, things are gonna be different. Whatever it takes to keep you loving me, I'll do it.' Even then, I still wasn't convinced, but he said he wanted to take care of me and that he loved me. So I tested him. I said, 'As much as Sharon?' and he was really struggling, I could see.

At last he said, 'No, not yet, but I do love you and it's getting there. You just gotta give me a little more time.' It hurt, hearing that, but at least I knew he was being totally honest. Then he said, 'I want to be with you now. If Sharon came back, I wouldn't have her, I'd choose you. Give me one last chance. I promise you, this time I'll make you happy.'

So here I am.

1 January 1998

Another New Year, another New Start. This time last year I was at B's, begging Grant to take me back. This year I ended up at B's again and it was Grant begging *me* to come back. Makes a change I suppose. I mean, at least I'm back on my terms. I've won, but at a price. Like I told Grant, he's destroyed something, that special thing I really loved about him. Now I know what he's capable of and it scares me. After the christening I told him I knew all his bad sides and that I didn't care, I loved him anyway. But now I've grown up a bit I realise I do care. I've got more self-respect.

Grant's on his best behaviour, tiptoeing round me like I'm made of china. I ain't letting him sleep with me, he's on the floor in the living-room. He brought me breakfast in bed this morning, with a rose on the tray and everything, and he ran my bath, but it'll take more than that to show me he's changed. I said to him, 'Don't think just because I'm here, everything's back to how it was.' I'm gonna keep him to his promises. He stood up to Aunt Sal for me later and he was polite to Simon, so it shows he's trying.

The worst thing now is that B ain't speaking to me. I know what she thinks about me being back with Grant, but he's my husband, and it's my life. She should be backing me up, not giving me a hard time. She came in the Vic earlier and had a right go. I said, 'You're my friend, you're supposed to understand,' and she went, 'Friend? You must be joking,' and walked out. I feel as if I've lost her and I don't know what to do. I can't give up Grant, but B's like a sister to me. Who else have I got?

6 January 1998

Me and B's still fighting. We had another row yesterday and I told her to mind her own business. She's carrying on like she's the one that's been hurt. I mean, I'm the one with a dirty great gash on me head! Then she had the nerve to tell Simon what happened on Boxing Day when I'd asked her to keep her big mouth shut. He came in and gave me the third degree, so now I'm getting it in the neck from both of 'em.

OK, so I used to tell him he shouldn't put up with Howard's violence, but that was different. Howard just wanted to control him. Grant really loves me and I know he don't mean to react the way he does. It's up to me to help him change. We can get our marriage sorted, it just might take a little time.

To be honest, I'm still a bit nervous of him, though I tried not to show it in front of Simon. Grant saw us arguing in the bar and came over. He said, 'What's going on?' in that hard voice of his, which made me flinch. I couldn't help it. Don't think Si noticed, though, thank goodness.

7 January 1998

Grant was as good as his word today. He persuaded Peggy to let me have more of a say in the running of the pub. I might even computerise all our accounts! Like I said to him, it's not that I wanna be working here all me life – I don't think the sun rises and sets because of the Queen Vic, even if him and Peggy do – but it's nice to feel I'm contributing.

8 January 1998

Talking about computers got me thinking about a new career. So this morning I went down the library and picked up a prospectus for Walford Tech. I was really surprised at all the courses you can do. Seeing as I used to work as a beautician, I thought it would be good to go for something along those lines. Then I saw this part-time course in body massage and it just leapt right out the page at me! (My boyfriends have always told me I've got 'magic hands'.) I wasn't sure what Grant would say about it, but he was really encouraging, so I went and signed up there and then. How's that for taking the initiative?

PS: Me and Grant are sleeping together again now. He's even making more of an effort in that department, too!!!

9 January 1998

Got me massage oils today. The lavender one smells gorgeous and I've got geranium and ylang-ylang (don't ask me how to say that) and sandalwood, which is supposed to be sexy. Grant took one sniff and said I could get some practice in on him. I'm pleased to say it works! (Not that I'll be doing that kind of massage! This is aromatherapy, it's all about healing and relaxing people.)

Afterwards, when we was up and dressed, he said, 'Tiffany, I've got something for you,' and reached in his pocket and pulled out a little box. I opened it and there was this beautiful diamond eternity ring. I didn't know what to say, and Grant went, 'You hate it, don't you? I'm sorry, it was a stupid idea,' and I said, 'No, no, I love it. It's just that you've taken me by surprise, that's all.' Then he said, 'I just want to show you how much you mean to me. Read what's inside.' I looked and it said, 'Tiffany, Forever Yours, Grant'. Romantic or what? I was so touched, I started to cry, and he gave me a big hug and held me for ages. It felt so right.

PS. Helped to look after Ian Beale's kids today, while he was in court with Cindy. She got a two-year conditional discharge for abducting the kids, but Ian slagged off the judge and was sent down for being in contempt. Everyone in the Square's talking about it. Kathy's furious.

13 January 1998

Made it up with B, at last. I'm so pleased. It's been horrible not speaking to each other. I passed her in the market and she said, 'Let's just forget what's happened, eh?' But I couldn't let it drop just like that. I mean, she tried to ruin my marriage. If I'd listened to her, me and Courtney would be by ourselves today, and as it is, we're back at home and really happy. We had a bit of a barney, but in the end we agreed to disagree. I've just gotta accept that she'll never like Grant. I can understand why. It must be difficult to see what makes our marriage work, looking at it from the outside. But then she don't know what I know. Grant's a different person when we're alone together. He's a real pussycat.

10 February 1998

Nothing much has happened recently, unless you count the community play. Pat and Peggy had a right old ding-dong at the first rehearsal and Pat resigned – well, abdicated actually – from her role as Queen Victoria. I reckon Peggy was just stirring it because she had her eye on the part, but Julie, the director, gave it to Pauline Fowler instead. I play Mrs Fossett, the mother of a large Walford family. Lots of lines and I sing, too! I'll have to start practising in the bath. Grant ain't in it, he thinks it's too poncy.

When I said nothing's been happening, I meant until today. This evening, me and Simon and Tony and Sarah was all summoned by Dad. I was a bit worried because I thought it might be to do with his health, you know? But he's only gone and proposed to Irene, hasn't he? And she's said yes (mad cow) and they're acting like a couple of giddy teenagers. Poor old Si don't know what to do. It means him and Tony are gonna be brothers-in-law!

12 March 1998

Courtney's first birthday! One year old – and it's flown by. She's such a grown-up little thing now. She's almost walking, though she won't let go of the furniture at the moment. And she's a real Miss Chatterbox. Not that we can understand what she's going on about! She says 'Daddy', which makes Grant very proud, but since she's pointing at a lamppost or a dustbin, often as not, I think she's still got a way to go. Either that, or she's got a great sense of humour. I made her a special little birthday cake with a candle on it and we got her tons of presents – I think we bought up half the toyshop. Everything seems to play a squeaky tune, which is driving me and Grant up the wall, but, of course, Courtney loves it!

17 March 1998

Why is it that people who don't deserve it get lucky? I'd be the first to admit Dad's a scrounger. He's been borrowing off me and Simon and anybody who's stupid enough to lend him a tenner. Then he goes and loses it all down the bookies. Normally. I told him I've had it with his gambling and I weren't gonna shell out no more, and he promised to stop. Next thing you know, he comes waltzing into the Vic with Irene on his arm and says, 'A bottle of your finest champagne, please,' and slings down this huge wad of notes on the bar. Thirty thousand pounds he won, on an accumulator bet! Irene looks like the cat that got the cream. All I can say is, I hope she's still smiling after they're married and Dad shows his true colours.

2 April 1998

Something's going on with Grant and Kathy. I dunno what – he won't talk to me about it. They was having this conversation in a corner of the bar yesterday, heads together, faces all serious, then today I saw her get in his car and they drove off somewhere. He came back quite a lot later and his face was like a mask. Course, he didn't say anything, so I asked, 'How did it go with Kathy?' And he jumped and looked really guilty. I said, 'Why the hush-hush date?' and he went, 'It's not what you think.' But since he won't say what's going on, what am I supposed to think? All I got was, 'It's nothing to do with you, so leave it.' But his voice…he was really cut up, I could tell. I hate being shut out.

10 April 1998

Well, Kathy left Walford today. She and Ben have gone to stay with her brother, Ted, in South Africa. For some reason, it feels like a weight's been lifted off my shoulders. It ain't logical, I know. I mean, there's no point in torturing meself thinking something was going on with her and Grant. She's pretty old – mid-forties at least – and he's hardly gonna fancy her when he's got a wife of 21, is he? It's just that I can't forget what Phil said when we was in Paris. I know he was drunk, but all the same…

Grant was in such a weird mood all day. He was right nasty to Peggy this morning, just cos she asked him to get Phil to try and talk Kathy out of going. She's desperate not to lose Ben cos he's her only grandson. I took Grant a coffee later and tried to get him to open up, but he ignored me. I said, 'Is it something I've done?' but he acted like I weren't there. It really upset me.

When I came downstairs, ten minutes later, he was on the phone, but he put it down the second he saw me. I asked him who he was calling but he wouldn't tell me. I said, 'Why's it such a big deal?' and he said, 'Cos of the way you're asking,' and then he went into this rant about my voice and how he was sick and tired of listening to it. I knew he was trying to put me off, so I went, 'Oh, I'm sorry but there's not much I can do about that. So do you mind telling me who you was phoning, O lord, O master?' He just flipped and punched the banisters and snapped one of them like a matchstick. Then he went striding out and I shouted after him, 'What were you doing, phoning her anyway?' cos I guessed who it was, but I don't think he heard me. But Peggy saw him go over to Kathy's, so I was right.

He was still being off with me later, and when I asked him if he'd persuaded Kathy to stay, he just said, 'She's having problems making up her mind.' He apologised after lunch, though. I found him upstairs, looking at Courtney asleep in her cot. He had this kinda sad expression on his face and when he saw me he said, 'I'm sorry. Not just for this morning. For everything.' I gave him a big kiss and said, 'What we gonna do about you and your temper, eh? I'd be lost without you. You know that, don't ya?' and he held me really tight.

Course, that didn't stop him going out and leaving me and Peggy in the lurch later on. He said he needed to go out and get some paint for the new banister he'd bought, but he was away for hours. The pump on the lager wouldn't work and neither of us could fix it, so I was dead relieved when he walked back in. We only found out later there had been all this drama over at Phil's with that woman Lorna taking an overdose. Grant and Phil had to rush her to hospital, then Grant had to stay to give them her details because Phil wanted to catch Kathy before her flight left. I don't think he made it in time though. Shame, innit?

14 April 1998

Courtney took her first proper steps today! Grant had taken the dog out, so he didn't see it. He'll be really disappointed. He's been going on about how stupid Phil was to ever get involved with Lorna – apparently, he missed seeing Ben learn to walk because he was bonking her at the time – and now Grant's missed Courtney's first steps, too. Still, at least Grant ain't got anyone else on the go. Mind you, he has been out a lot lately. He keeps dragging the dog off for walks along the canal, plus he's got that look on his face – what I call his 'bulldog sucking a lemon' expression. Don't know what's got into him, he's dead moody these days.

Goss update – Cindy Beale's been arrested for Ian's shooting. She was behind it all along. The old bill turned up and nabbed her just as she was about to take custody of their kids a few days ago. Word is, she'll go down for a long stretch. She's pregnant, too, by that smarmy boyfriend of hers. He won't have nothing to do with her now, though. What kind of a start is her poor baby gonna have?

16 April 1998

Big day today – the community play. I think it went quite well, considering, though there was a few hiccups. Sonia, Josh and Martin, who were supposed to be playing my kids, missed their cue and me and Alex had to improvise – but not as much as Peggy, who was brilliant when Pat forgot her lines. She brought the house down! Bianca set up Ricky after we found out he was behind her costumes getting nicked. He said it was an April Fool's joke that got out of hand, but B didn't see the funny side of it and neither did I. So just before he went on for the fashion parade at the end we told him his costume was missing and made him dress up as a girl. Ricky in a mini-skirt! I'd've paid to see that alone.

Peggy had organised a bit of a knees-up at the Vic afterwards, but when I saw her she looked a bit tense. I think she'd had a fight with George cos he left early, looking really down. I'd put money on Grant and Phil having a hand in it, but as usual I'm the last to be told anything around here.

21 April 1998

Went to the opening of Giuseppe's, that new Italian restaurant in Turpin Road that George owns. Loads of people turned up and there was a really good atmosphere. Had a nice time chatting with the two brothers. Gianni and Beppe they're called.

Very good-looking! Gianni works there, and Beppe's in the police, though he don't look like any copper I've ever met. They was making a bit of a fuss of me, getting me drinks and stuff – pretty harmless, you know? But Grant being Grant gets into one of his strops. First of all, he's rude to Gianni, barging in and going, 'Why don't you go and do the washing up?' Then he accuses me of flirting with them both and drags me out the restaurant. It was so humiliating. In front of all those people! I said to him, 'I'm warning you, if you ever touch me again… Well, he knows what I'd do. I'm not hanging around to be treated like that again. I've been there and I swore I wasn't going back, and I meant it. I think he got the message.

22 April 1998

Me and Grant ain't speaking. Peggy's freezing him out too, but that's because Grant and Phil both knew about George being a crook and they kept it from her till the other day. Apparently, George is up to his neck in it, big time, and he's got some dangerous enemies. They've already torched his flat. His daughter Annie's in on it, too. Not only that, but Phil's gone into business with her, debt-collecting. That's how it all went wrong. They used George's name and then this other gang got wind of what they was up to and came after George. It's really frightening. I mean, what if they'd fired the Vic while he was staying here? Peggy's broke up with him, but I know she's miserable about it cos she really loves George.

23 April 1998

I never thought I'd see it happen, but Grant hit Peggy today. His own mother! She's only a little thing and he's this great big bull, but he slapped her round the face really hard. Poor Peggy's still in shock. She told him to get out and he has. That was at eight o'clock. It's now half-past midnight and he ain't come back.

He'd been acting strange all day. Well, if I'm honest, he's been acting strange for ages now. We had a set-to this morning and he was accusing me of doing his head in! He was carrying on about the business at the restaurant and I went, 'Do you really think if I was gonna flirt, I'd be stupid enough to do it in front of you?' And he goes, 'Well, at least Boxing Day taught you something.' It completely took my breath away. I could hardly believe my ears.

Later, we was working in the bar and Grant started on at me again about the Di Marcos (that's their surname, Beppe and Gianni), then he began slagging off Dad. I said, 'Don't make out you're so wonderful. Your first wife never left you because you were such a teddy bear,' and he went bananas because I'd mentioned the sacred Sharon. He hauled me through to the back and goes, 'Sharon's got nothing to do with you,' and I went, 'No? How many Boxing Day presents did you give her?' He was white with rage and I could see he was close to losing it. He got me by the shoulders and went, 'Do you want to talk about this upstairs?' I was beginning to feel really scared but then Peggy came through to the hallway. She yelled at Grant to let go of me, which he did, eventually. He stormed off upstairs and she followed him. I just stood there, shaking like a leaf. Then I heard them both shouting and I thought I'd better go up, make sure Peggy was OK. I got to the doorway of the living-room and they was having a right old ding-dong. Peggy was telling him he had nothing going for him but his fists and that he weren't fit to be a father. He just turned round and walloped her.

I don't think he can face her now. It's like he's committed the ultimate sin – as if pushing me around weren't bad enough. She's alright, though she's got a bit of a mark there. But I don't know where any of us go from here.

27 April 1998

Not a word from Grant all weekend. We know he's hiding out at Phil's cos Phil ain't shown his face either. I told Peggy I should go round to talk to him, but at first she weren't having it. Then Grant sent Nigel round with a list to pick up a load of his belongings and I knew it was serious. I've finally managed to persuade Peggy to let me go round to Phil's and I'm off in a minute. After all, Grant needs me. He can talk to me about stuff he can't talk to Peggy or Phil about. And I need him. I still want to make our marriage work. We just gotta find a way to deal with his temper, that's all. He'll listen to me, I know he will.

11.30pm: Grant's leaving. He's on a plane right now, flying to Cyprus to stay with some army mate of his. Don't know how long he's going away for. He don't know himself. I feel numb. How can he do that? Just walk out of our lives as if me and Courtney don't mean anything to him? I wouldn't even have known if I hadn't gone over to see him. He was coming out the door with his bags packed, trying to sneak off without saying a word to us.

He said he wanted to get away from the Square, away from his family, that he was stifled here and there was no one he could talk to. That made me so angry. After all we've been through! I stood in his way and said, 'Come on, you want someone to talk to, I'm here, talk to me. Ever since Easter it's been like you weren't really here.' All he said was, 'Kathy said she thought I could change. I don't know if I can.' I went, 'What's she got to do with it?' I mean, she's in Cape Town now, for crying out loud. He goes, 'She said maybe I could get through all the bad stuff and start again.'

That hurt because suddenly I knew what all those little conversations were about – Grant discussing our relationship with Kathy, Albert Square's agony aunt. I know she worked for the Samaritans once, but that still don't give her the right to stick her nose into our private business. I told Grant I didn't want to hear about her, I wanted to hear about him and me, but he shook his head and said, 'Whatever I touch I end up wrecking it. Just let me go.' I begged him not to, but he wouldn't listen.

He said, 'I'm doing this for you and Mum and Courtney.' And then he left. Just like that.

Courtney's sleeping with me at the moment. I'm looking at her now, lying on Grant's side of the bed. She's fast asleep, her face so innocent and peaceful. I don't understand how Grant could leave her. She's his little princess, 'Daddy's favourite girl' he calls her. Whatever him and me's been through, he would never desert her. That's why I feel so afraid. What if he don't come back? What am I gonna tell her? What has she done to deserve any of this?

30 April 1998

My head's in such a muddle. I feel so helpless, just sitting around here, waiting. What if Grant meets someone else in Cyprus? Someone more mature? Perhaps that's what he really wants. I mean, if he got on with Kathy that well... I overheard Phil talking to Peggy about Grant today. She was saying he should have tried harder to make things work, and Phil said, 'Maybe Grant don't want to.' I collared Phil later in the bar and asked him if Grant was seeing someone else, but he didn't seem to know any more than me.

We had a send-off party for Nigel in the bar tonight. He's moving to Scotland to be with Julie. He's so sweet. He came to say goodbye and told me that if I still had feelings for Grant, I should stick around and give it another chance. He gave me a cuddle and it felt so nice to be comforted. I'll really miss him. At least Nigel's found happiness. If anyone deserves it, he does.

11 May 1998

I think that Beppe's trying to make a pass at me. He's the older brother, the copper, the one with eyes like molten chocolate. He was chatting me up in the market the other day, then today he comes in the Vic with this CD for me. Opera music, if you please! I said, 'Crikey, I don't know the first thing about it,' but he was going on about how passionate it was. He said, 'I know I come across as a bit of a tough nut, but when I get home from work I sit down and put on some opera and I go all weak and romantic,' which made me giggle. He told me to listen to this particular track – 'One Fine Day', it's called. I put it on the stereo later and I was really getting into it when the phone goes and it's Grant. Course, Peggy tells him I'm listening to Beppe's CD and he goes mad straight off, carrying on about me behaving myself. I said, 'Me behave myself! You've got some front, after the way you disappeared.' After that, it weren't a very long conversation.

14 May 1998

What a bloomin' disaster my family is. I never could bring me friends home when I was young cos Mum and Dad would always end up having a flaming row and embarrassing me. Well, nothing's changed. Just as I get meself settled and start putting down some roots, Mum turns up and does it again. And it ain't as if she's come back to see me and Simon, I bet. She's sniffing around after Dad's money.

Anyways, she walked in on Dad and Irene's wedding. There was the vicar, about to proclaim them husband and wife, and Mum bursts into the church and says, 'Oh, no you don't. Terry Raymond is still married to me.' Well, there was this gasp from everybody and Irene went white as a sheet. Apparently, Dad had told her him and me mum was never officially married! Whereas he'd told us they'd been divorced for years.

I could hardly take it in. I mean, we ain't seen her for nearly ten years, then she makes this barnstorming entrance back into our lives without a word of warning. I felt so muddled up, seeing her again. All of a sudden, I felt like a little kid. Only I'm not, I'm a grown woman with a husband and child of my own. I've got on with me life without her. I've had to. I dunno how many times I've told meself I don't need her, but as soon as I saw her, it all kinda crumbled and I just wanted her to hold me. But there she was, making this big public scene and ignoring me and Si. It made me feel so angry and upset. I just couldn't take it and ran outside, crying me eyes out.

Beppe came out and was comforting me, then he offered to give me a lift home cos I said there was no way I was gonna go to the reception, even if everybody else was. He came upstairs to make sure I was alright and got me a brandy. I must've looked awful, mascara everywhere and me nose all red. I ended up telling him all about Mum walking out on us when we was younger and he was really understanding. Then he went, 'If I thought for a minute you'd say yes, I'd take you away from here.' He said he knew this place, a villa in Italy with beautiful views where no one would hassle us. I said, 'It sounds wonderful, but you're not really gonna ask me, are you?' I felt his breath on my cheek and his face was really close. He whispered, 'We could always pretend. You must know how I feel about you.' It made me tingle all over, the way he looked into my eyes. I so wanted to be kissed and held, what with everything that's gone on and feeling so vulnerable, that I nearly gave in. But at the last moment I came to me senses. I told him, 'I think I've got enough on me plate without cheating on me husband,' and showed him the door. But I get the feeling he ain't gonna give up easily.

18 May 1998

Mum came round to the Vic today, expecting me and her to kiss and make up for years in half an hour. I told her exactly what I thought of her selfish behaviour, clearing off and leaving me and Si to take the flak from Dad. She said she was sorry and suggested we all go out for a meal before she goes home. It'll take more than a bowl of spag bol and a bottle of house red to change how I feel about her, but I suppose I might as well go.

19 May 1998

Just had a huge bust-up with Mum. We went out to Giuseppe's and it was going quite well until she started criticising our relationships. First she had a go at Simon for getting involved with his new boyfriend, Chris, who she met last night. Says he's unreliable and not to be trusted. Then she had a go at me about Grant – who she ain't even met – because I admitted to her we was going through a bad patch. I said, 'Oh, so everybody should do what you did, eh? Go swanning off and leave your kids to fend for themselves,' and it went downhill from there. We'd all had a few too many glasses of wine, which didn't help, and Mum got really upset. I don't think the Di Marcos were too happy with us cos we left without eating anything.

21 May 1998

Mum went home today, back to her toyboy – Gary, his name is. Simon says he's about half her age. Still, Mum looks pretty good for nearly 40. I'd put her at least five years younger, maybe more. She looks after herself and she dresses young. (A bit too young, I think – like she's trying too hard.) Still, she's obviously got what it takes to have the fellas queuing up.

I'm glad we made up before she left. I went round to see her at Simon's this morning and apologised. She said it was OK, she didn't blame me for being angry with her and that she'd never forgiven herself either for what she did. Reading between the lines, I think she's had a really hard time, living with the guilt. I felt sad when she went. There was so much I wanted to tell her about, so much she don't know – about me and Grant and about Courtney (she's right put out at being a grand-mother!). Still, she promised to stay in touch. I hope next time I see her, me and Grant'll be back together and she can see what a happy family her grown-up daughter's got.

3 June 1998

Phil had the nerve to show his face in the Vic today. He said was I alright? I goes, 'Fine, thanks, apart from having my baby threatened by gangsters.' I've still got the jitters, thinking about what could have happened to Courtney. I haven't let her out of my sight since Monday night. I ain't even been outside in case they're still out there and they try and grab her or something. I'm jumping at the slightest little noise, I lie in bed going hot and cold, thinking I can hear footsteps on the landing...it's a nightmare. I'm so frightened. I wish Grant was here.

It's all Phil's fault for getting involved in that protection racket with Annie Palmer. These thugs came to the Vic looking for George, and when they didn't find him with Peggy, they went over and put the screws on Phil. He was babysitting Courtney for me cos I'd gone out with Mary and Ruth and Polly and a few others to see Mick's band at the Titanic Cat. We went on to a party and by the time we got back it was really late. I assumed Peggy had collected Courtney cos Phil wasn't answering the door. When she told us about the creeps who'd threatened her, I felt the hairs stand up on the back of me neck. We rushed round to Phil's flat and Mary squeezed in through the front window. My heart was thumping so fast. I was terrified of what we'd find. Courtney was lying on the floor next to Phil, who was tied up, and for one awful moment I thought... God I'm blubbing again and the ink's running...Well, I thought the worst. But she was there, fast asleep. Phil said they hadn't touched her. He'd been beaten up, but not as bad as Annie Palmer. They did her over good and proper. She's in hospital. See why I'm so scared?

12 June 1998

Feeling really low today. I had this dream last night that Grant wasn't gonna come home – ever. He's been away seven weeks now. Feels as if my life's going down the plughole. Bianca told me off for being so miserable, but I told her it weren't that – I was just feeling old before my time. I mean, there we was, getting the bar all decked out for Roy Evans's 63rd birthday party, and it's the highlight of my week. Nothing like life in the fast lane! The only thing that made it fun was Gianni and Beppe, who are still giving me the eye. Peggy told them to stop drooling on her bar but I think Phil was a bit more up front with them!

15 June 1998

Well, Grant's back. He phoned yesterday to tell us he was coming and he arrived early this morning. My dream must have been a sort of omen in reverse! I'm pleased he's home, though I ain't showing it to him. If he thinks I'm gonna welcome him back with open arms, he can think again. I know I can cope without him cos I've had to, whether it's been changing light bulbs or bringing up Courtney. I'm stronger now. This time, I'm taking him back on my terms. And for starters, he's sleeping on the sofa again until I decide otherwise.

He's been making a huge fuss of Courtney, saying about how much she's grown and her hair's longer and all. I said, what did he expect after two months? I mean, she can feed herself with a spoon now. He said how much he'd missed her and he'd thought about us a lot while he was away, and I went, 'Well, it's a pity you didn't think about her before you decided to push off to Cyprus.' I mean, he can make excuses about how it was the best thing for everybody, but like I told him, 'At the end of the day, you walked out and deserted your wife and child.'

It was Mary who let slip about what happened the other night with those thugs. I knew Grant would find out eventually, so I told him the whole story. Course, he was furious with Phil and was all set to go over and sort him out when Peggy comes in and gives him a flea in his ear. She told him to leave well alone, but I saw him sneak out later and I knew where he was going. Luckily, Phil weren't in.

Anyways, Grant weren't the only wanderer to return today. Mum turned up, too. Apparently, she's split up with Gary and she's gonna stay in Walford for a while. I brought Grant over to meet her and they both looked a bit embarrassed and said they'd already met! Seems they ran into each other outside Giuseppe's this morning. Small world, innit?

16 June 1998

I really think Grant is trying to change. He and Phil have settled their differences without killing each other, and he even managed to restrain himself when Beppe started flirting with me. It don't do no harm to show Grant other men find me attractive, so I went along with it. Grant's face was a picture. Perhaps he won't be so quick to go running off and leaving me alone in future. Cos if he does, I won't be waiting around when he gets back.

26 June 1998

Heard back about a massage course I applied for – there's been a cancellation and I can go! They've got a creche, so I can take Courtney, too. I told Grant, thinking he might be a bit sticky about it, but he said, 'Whatever makes you happy.' Course, he weren't even bothering to listen to me properly, was he? Cos today, when I reminded him about it, he went ballistic. I said I was gonna go whatever he said – I mean, it's only for a couple of weeks, and he went off to Cyprus for two months – and anyway, it's my career. I'm serious about being a masseuse. Even so, his attitude's depressing me. He obviously ain't interested in what I want to do. It's like he's just going through the motions.

29 June 1998

The timetable came through for my course today. Sounds really interesting. We have to learn about all sorts of things – circulation, allergies, lymphatic drainage, whatever that is. Peggy was dead impressed. I did a practise massage on her later, a proper one with relaxing music and warm towels and everything. She loved it. She made Grant come up after her, but he was really grumpy about it. He was all tense and he kept going on about how he weren't happy with me doing this to other blokes. I told him I'd only done women so far and he thought that was weird an' all. Then he had the nerve to suggest I should've taken up sewing instead! I says, 'I'd watch it because the position you're in right now I wouldn't go upsetting me,' then I had a right good go at his shoulders! Peggy and Phil crept upstairs to watch, which of course only made Grant more cross, and he got up and stormed off, all covered in oil. He used to love my massages. I can't think why he's got such a bee in his bonnet about this.

1 July 1998

We've had a right set-to in here today. First of all, Dad comes in shouting his mouth off because Irene's found out about his past. I felt a bit guilty cos Sarah was sticking her nose in a few days ago and me and Mum and Simon decided to put her straight about Dad. She told Irene and now Irene's given him the boot. He drunk himself stupid in here all day, then fell off his barstool and passed out. Grant had to cart him off upstairs to sleep it off. Then Irene came in and she looked terrible, eyes all red and puffy. She asked me if it was true about what Dad did to me. I guess my expression said it all cos she looked upset and went straight out again. As it is, she and Mum are at daggers drawn. It's mascara wands at fifty paces whenever they come within spitting distance. Happy families, eh?

2 July 1998

Bumped into Beppe and little Joe, his son, at the playground today. We sat on the swings and talked for a bit while the two children played. He told me a bit about his marriage and why it had gone wrong. It was really freaky – it could have been me and Grant he was describing, our situations are so similar.

I like Beppe, he's sweet and he listens and he's kind. If it wasn't for Grant...but there you go. We've got to stick with working at our marriage. I'm sure things'll get better in time. It's Grant's birthday next Wednesday and I'm planning something really special for him. Peggy wanted to do it, but I insisted. We're all going out to this fantastic French restaurant, and I've ordered a cake, too. Only thing is, I don't know what to get him as a present. Still thinking about that one.

6 July 1998

Everything's going wrong. I don't think I can take much more of Grant's behaviour. Thank God for the massage course. I can't wait to get away. That's half the trouble, Grant don't want me to go on it. There's a party at the end and he's sulking in advance. He's so jealous of me being with other men, but what he don't realise is, if he gave me more attention, I wouldn't flirt with them. Not that I do, really, it's just that it's nice to have a giggle now and again. Beppe was in this lunchtime and we was chatting, about childcare actually, cos Courtney's teething and she had me up four times last night. Grant came over and made a right idiot of himself, dragging me away and yelling at me to behave.

I ignored him for the rest of the day, then this evening, just as I was getting ready to go out – I'd arranged to meet B and Ricky at the opening of the new Night Café – Grant comes in and says he wants to talk. He tells me he's booked tickets for me and him and Courtney to fly to Scotland and stay at Nigel's. Only thing was, it was the same week as me massage course. I said, 'Grant, I know you're trying to make an effort, but this ain't the way, alright?' Cos there was no way I was cancelling the course. Then I went out. Blow me if he didn't come chasing over to the café five minutes later and haul me out, shoving some bloke over in the process. He was trying to put me on the spot, making out it was a choice between him or 'that poxy massage course' as he calls it. I told him I was going on it and that was that, and went back inside with me head held high.

7 July 1998

I found Grant sorting through his old army photos this morning. Pictures of him in the Falklands, back in 1982. He looked so young and keen – boyish. And he had hair! He looked really smart in his uniform. I spotted it hanging on the back of the wardrobe door, so he must have been having a sort-out.

He never talks about it, what he did then. I told him I was curious – I mean, there's whole chunks of his life I know nothing about – but he didn't say much, just that he liked army life cos it was simple and you knew what was expected of you. I said, 'And that was enough?' and he went, 'I was happy,' giving me this look that says, 'and now I ain't'. I told him we was in a rut and that's why I'm doing me massage and that he should do something an' all. It could be a fresh start for the both of us. I left him thinking about it and he came back later and said it was a good idea. We had a kiss and made up and then he went off out saying he was going to the brewery.

He was away hours and when he got back I took one look and knew he was in a stinking mood. It's the way he carries his shoulders all hunched and lowers his head like a battering ram, you know? I was in the bar with Mum and Mary and Peggy and Beppe and we was having a little joke about Grant's age cos he's 36 tomorrow. Mary said, 'Even my dad's younger than him,' and Grant went, 'Shut your mouth,' and stomped off, leaving her in tears.

I found him upstairs, staring at his army stuff again. He wouldn't tell me what was wrong. He just said, 'What's the point? I can't be a different person for you and you can't be a different person for me.' Then he told me to cancel his birth-day meal because he didn't feel like celebrating. I was really upset cos I wanted to make it a special day for him, and he went, 'Tiffany, stop kidding yourself. There is no fresh start. It just ain't gonna happen.'

So where does that leave us? I haven't a clue cos he's spent the rest of the evening drinking and won't talk to me. I'm beginning to feel desperate.

9 July 1998

My life's a disaster. If it wasn't for Courtney…well, I don't know what I'd do. But I've got to get my act together, for her sake. It's not as if her daddy's gonna be there for her all the time. Not any more. From now on, it's up to me. I haven't worked out how we'll manage, yet – it's too much to think about right at the moment. All I know is, me and Grant are fin-ished. For good.

It all happened at Grant's birthday meal. He'd had a change of heart about celebrating his birthday – don't ask me why – but it was too late to get another reservation, so we ended up at Giuseppe's. Things got off to a bad start, with everyone winding Grant up about me massaging nude men. Then George and Frank and Ricky came in for some sort of business dinner and Peggy couldn't handle seeing George again and got plas-tered and fell over. Grant was carrying on as if I'm gonna be running some kind of bordello from the Vic, making cracks about red lights and rubber sheets. Him and Mum had words and he said he didn't care what I did any more, which made me feel about two inches high. And then he opened my present and went totally ape.

See, I thought it would be a really nice idea to get him a book about the Falklands, since it obviously means so much to him. I had to walk miles before I found this one. 'Falklands – The Real War' it's called. Lots of pictures an' stuff. I thought it would take him back, you know? But when he unwrapped it, he got this weird expression on his face and shouted, 'You stupid little bitch.' It went completely silent and the whole restaurant was looking at us. Then he yelled, 'You ain't got the faintest idea, have you? You was still at school then. But I killed people out there. My best mates died out there. Do you really think I want to be reminded of all that?'

I was so shocked that I just got up and ran out. He might as well have hit me in front of everyone cos that's what it felt like – another slap in the face. And the state he was in, I knew he would give me the real thing when we got home. That's when I realised I had to leave. I rushed back to the Vic and told Bianca, who was babysitting, to take Courtney to her place, then I stuffed a few things in a bag. I was trying to get out before Grant got back, but it was too late.

Funnily enough, I wasn't scared this time. It was like I could see him for what he was, at last. I said, 'It's over Grant. Fact is, you don't love me, you never have, only you ain't got the courage to admit it, so you try and push me around and humiliate me. It ain't even me you hate, it's yourself, cos you haven't got the guts to end it. Well, I've had enough. You can hit me, you can do what you want because I don't care. I'm leaving you and this time I ain't never coming back.' Then I walked out.

13 July 1998

I'm stopping at Ruth's at the moment, kipping on the sofa with Courtney on a mattress on the floor. Mum's staying here and Ruth has been very kind about putting us up as well. I didn't like to impose on B for more than one night. She didn't say nothing, but we've been there too many times before. Mind you, Mum's driving me absolutely nuts already. She keeps going on and on about Grant cos she thinks I'm gonna go back to him. B does an' all. They both think I'm weak. Well, I

'We'll always have Paris.' Good memories for me and Grant, lousy ones for Kathy and Phil on our post-Blessing holiday in France. Ricky and Bianca stayed with Ricky's sister, Diane (sitting between me and B).

A caring, sharing marital discussion. Not!

Courtney and I go to cheer up Bianca.

Girls just wanna have fun. Me and B, set to party.

Unwedded bliss: Dad and Irene, his bride-who-wasn't-to-be, before his attempted bigamy was exposed by Mum.

Grant wasn't best pleased about me going on a three-week residential massage course, but I was determined to make a career for myself.

Top: Italian stallions Beppe (left) and Gianni di Marco make a fuss of me.
Below: Grant's 36th birthday party at Giuseppe's was a total disaster.

Mum struts her funky stuff at the opening of the Night Café.

Mum and I got really close again for a time.

Surprise! Grant turned up uninvited when me and Mum had a party to celebrate our birthdays. It all worked out OK in the end, though . . .

. . . but not before I was almost tempted to sleep with Beppe. I didn't cos it made me realise it was Grant I really loved.

Mum tries to do what she does best – run away again, without telling me. I was really angry at first, but I finally managed to talk her into staying.

showed 'em. I stood up to him in front of the whole pub and I humiliated him like he's always humiliating me.

I only went round to get the rest of my stuff, not to have a full-scale row. Peggy had sent Grant off to the Cash and Carry to keep him out the way, but he got back just as I was leaving. He said he wanted to talk, so I said OK, but all he did was ramble on about this mid-life crisis he's having, not a word of an apology. He got turned down by the Territorial Army, which was what sent him over the top. I went, 'Is that all?' and he goes, 'It's not a very nice thing not to be wanted.' I was flabbergasted! I stood up and said, 'There's just one thing. You haven't mentioned me.' Then I walked out.

Well, he came belting down the stairs after me and started demanding all my things back cos he said he'd paid for them. It was pathetic, really pathetic. I mean, I've worked behind that bar, night after night, I've earned everything I own. And more, considering what I've had to put up with from Grant. Talk about blood money! I took off my rings and said, 'Here. You did pay for these, and I don't want them any more.' I'm sure I heard someone cheer as I left the bar.

14 July 1998

Been feeling so down today – stupid, lonely, useless. A nothing, just like Grant always said I was. I wasn't going to go on the massage course, there didn't seem to be any point, but my family and friends have been really great encouraging me, and I'm feeling much more positive now. Ruth looked after Courtney while I went and did some shopping (having cleared out half of our joint account to tide me over) and Simon even threw a special dinner party to cheer me up. I don't think he enjoyed himself that much cos Chris, his boyfriend, brought his ex, Ali, along. But I had a good time and afterwards I decided I was gonna grab hold of life with both hands and go on me massage course after all. I mean, I gotta earn a living somehow,

I can hardly work at the Vic now, can I? So I've decided, this is gonna be the first day of the rest of my life. Watch out world, here I come! (Simon must've put something in the cheesecake...)

16 July 1998

I'm here, at the health farm. The course starts tomorrow. It feels strange, sitting in this neat little bedroom, knowing it's gonna be our home for the next three weeks. I feel lonely and a bit scared. Well, terrified, if I'm honest. There's so much to cope with. Learning all the theory, which I've never been good at, and then there's the massage itself. What if I don't pass? Everything's resting on it. This ain't just my future, it's Courtney's, too.

She's spark out beside me, though I had trouble getting her off to sleep – she was really over-excited. It's a lot for her to take in, poor lamb, all these changes of scene. It must be so confusing for her. One minute she's living in the Vic with her mum and dad, then she's camping on someone's floor, and now she's in a hotel room. She hasn't eaten much today and I'm sure it's because she's unsettled by it all.

I wanted Grant to see her before we left. I thought it was only fair. I don't want her being used as some sort of punchbag between us and whatever he's done to me, Grant's entitled to see Courtney. I left a message for him with Phil, telling him we was leaving at half-past four, but he didn't show. So that's how much he cares for his little girl. I don't know why I bothered.

11 August 1998

Well, I passed.The examiners said I did really well, I'm a natural. The coursework was hard – I've been up studying every night until midnight – but it was worth it. I've never achieved anything like this in me life. I'm so proud, I could burst! I can't describe how I feel. It's like I'm somebody, at last. Tiffany Mitchell, masseuse. I don't need to answer to nobody no more.

I can be me own boss, run me own business, make me own money. And what's so great is that I've fitted in, you know? I was worried the others would be a right stuck-up lot and they'd see me as this stupid little East End tart and we'd have nothing in common. But everyone's been fantastic. We get on really well and I've made loads of new friends. There's a party tonight and I can't wait. It'll be fab to let me hair down and boogie. I'm gonna go wild!

15 August 1998

Guess where I am? Spain! Marbella, to be precise. Me and the girls had such fun on the course, we decided to go away on holiday together afterwards. There's seven of us sharing this apartment, plus Courtney. Everyone's making a fuss of her and she's having a brilliant time, too.

I had to phone Mum to get me passport from the Vic. She said Grant was quite helpful, which surprised me. Still, I ain't thinking about him at the moment, or Albert Square or the British weather. I'm lazing about in the sun, drinking Moscow Mules and having a ball. Don't want to go home! Sent Bianca a postcard, telling her there was loads of gorgeous blokes chasing after me. Truth is, I ain't bothering with all these Spanish waiters giving me the eye, it's just that I thought I'd wind Grant up cos I know she won't be able to resist telling him!

24 August 1998

It's really strange being back in Walford. Everything looks so grey and tatty and dull here. I'm determined not to let it get to me though cos this is the new Tiffany talking. I've got a great tan, some new clothes and, most of all, I've got self-confidence. I feel like a million dollars. Judging by the looks Gianni was giving me when I went past him earlier, he thinks so too! B could see the difference straight off. She said I looked amazing. I told her the girls made me buy this dress. I thought it was too tarty, but they said I looked stunning in it. That's when I realised I've been listening to Grant for so long telling me how rubbish I am that I was beginning to believe it meself. It's only since I've left him that I've realised I'm not a bad mother or a horrible person. I know it's been a long time coming, but I'm finally rid of him now. And I've got a little surprise for him up me sleeve.

10.00pm: Went to see Grant this evening and told him I was gonna divorce him. No hysterics or nothing. Just dropped it into the conversation and strolled out. You should've seen his face! I ran into Beppe outside the Vic and he asked me out on a date. I wasn't sure, but then I saw Grant watching us, so I gave Beppe a kiss and said I'd love to. It means me and Mum will be dating brothers – turns out she's been seeing Gianni on the sly. She's a man-eater, that woman!

25 August 1998

Went out with Beppe this evening, to Giuseppe's. It was my idea. I didn't want to be too far away from Courtney until she's settled back in again. I don't think Beppe was very keen on going to his family's restaurant – Gianni and Teresa, their sister, was winding him up something chronic. We were both a bit nervous, but I had to laugh when Beppe put his sleeve in the soup. Then he told me it was Gianni's shirt and he'd go mad and we both started giggling. I had a nice time but I decided to be honest with him upfront. I told him I liked him but that I couldn't make any commitments, not just yet. He was really sweet and said, 'I've been on my own for a while now. I think I can wait a bit longer.' I hope he does.

27 August 1998

Me and Mum have moved into our own place today – the flat above the bookies in Turpin Road. It's small but we've made it nice. Mum's got a real talent for doing places up. You should have seen what she did to Ruth's. It seems so strange to be living with my mother again after all these years. It wouldn't be every daughter's cup of tea, but I'm loving it. We're really close now. I feel as if we can talk about anything.

31 August 1998

Gave Grant some times he could come and see Courtney. Like I told him, I want to do this properly, until we get the divorce sorted out. Unfortunately, Courtney decided to take a nap when he came round, which made things a bit awkward. Eventually, she woke up though and he took her out to the park, which she really enjoyed. She came back babbling 'Daddy this' and 'Daddy that'. Grant loved it, of course. I'd almost forgotten about his gentle side, but when I saw him with Courtney, it made me remember things. He's not all bad. There was a time when we was happy, although that seems a long way away now.

1 September 1998

Me and Beppe took the children to the swings this afternoon. I swear Little Joe was flirting with Courtney! Like father, like son. It wasn't a date as such, although Beppe looked really smart. He asked if we could go out again without the kids and I said 'maybe'. Beppe's a lovely bloke, it's just that my head's still so messed up over Grant that I can't handle anything heavy at the moment. Then, talk of the devil, Grant appeared – checking up on me, I'm sure – and said he wanted to take me out for a drink to go over some stuff. I suppose he means plans for Courtney once we're divorced. I thought no time like the present. So I said yes. I've got butterflies in me stomach about it already.

PS My massage table arrived today. It's huge!

2 September 1998

Grant wants me back. I'm still reeling from the shock of what he said to me this evening. He took me out to this wine bar and said he wanted us to make a fresh start, away from the Vic. He's been doing this secret deal to buy us the wine bar we was at. There's a flat above it and everything. It was all I ever wanted – before – somewhere of our own, just him, me and Courtney. Why couldn't he have done it then? It's too late now. I told him that. Changing the view won't change how he feels about me. We'd still be unhappy. Then he said that being apart had made him realise how much he loves me. It was so out of the blue I didn't know what to say. In the end, I agreed to think about it, but to be honest, my mind's in such a whirl I don't know what to do.

7 September 1998

Of course, I fell for it again. Grant wants to get out of the Vic alright – because Frank and Peggy are an item, that's why! Peggy told me Grant's feeling 'pushed out'. So what it boils down to is obviously a toss-up for Grant between looking at me or Frank over the breakfast table. Am I supposed to be flattered or something? Not only that, but Grant told Peggy I'd agreed to the wine bar business. There he is, trying to manipulate my life again, and we ain't even together. I should've known. A leopard can't change its spots. I'm so steaming mad at him, but at the same time...well, I can't change how I feel, either. Despite everything that's happened, I still love him. I've tried not to, but I can't help it. I knew he was what I was looking for when I married him and, last week, when he said he loved me, I felt like I could have that again. We belong together. I know it sounds daft, like one of those doomed romances – I mean, we ain't exactly Heathcliff and Cathy – but there you go. Que sera and all that. What will be, will be.

Everyone'll think I'm barking, of course. B's already had a

go at me and I know what Simon will say. Mum was OK about it though, when I discussed it with her. She said I had to do what was right for me, not listen to other people. I said to her, 'Mum, I've done it before. How many more chances should I give him?' and she said, 'When you love someone as much as you love Grant, I don't think it's even worth counting.'

8 September 1998

I decided to go over and see Grant this evening, have it all out with him, you know? But when it came to the crunch, I started to get cold feet. B told me I needed to organise things in me head, make it clear what I wanted from him so he couldn't confuse me, but it ain't easy. Once Grant starts talking I ain't able to think straight.

In the end, it was simpler to tell him what I didn't want. I said I didn't want to be ignored, I didn't want to be lied to and I didn't want to be abused for no reason. He promised to try his best, which was a good start. I also told him I wasn't going to do any more bar work cos I want to carry on with me massage business, which surprised him a bit but he agreed.

I thought we'd sorted it and I was feeling really pleased until I asked him one last small thing. I said I wanted Mum to move in as well. I mean, it ain't much, considering how long I've had to put up with his mum! And it would only be until she was earning enough to afford her own place. But Grant wouldn't even consider it. He went completely mad, shouting at me and being as pig-headed as ever. So I told him it was no go and that was that. From now on, I'm just gonna forget he ever existed.

10 September 1998

It's my birthday on Sunday, mine and Mum's. Simon's throwing a party for us. I feel like kicking the traces over, going a bit wild. I think I deserve to, after what Grant's put me through. I've invited Beppe and his brother, since Mum's still dating

Gianni. Not that she needs any help with her love life. I just wish she'd keep her nose out of mine. I caught her and Grant today, sneaking around in the Square with guilty looks on their faces. I know what they was up to cos Peggy told me Mum had been round to the Vic. She's cooking up some plan to get me to change my mind and go back to him. I told them both, they can forget it. I said no to Grant and I meant it.

14 September 1998

Phew! Where do I start? It was my birthday yesterday and I've ended up with the best present in the world. It could've turned out so differently, though. I shudder to think how close I came to losing everything.

We had the party at our flat. It started off with party games, then me and Mum opened our pressies and found that we'd given each other identical little black dresses. Funny that. I mean, I know she's 40 and I'm 22, but we have the same taste in loads of things. She's got a real hang-up about her age, but I think she looks great and Gianni obviously thinks so, too. She's kept her figure really well. I hope I can get away with what she does when I'm her age.

Anyway, the best present was Simon's. He'd got hold of Dad's old projector, one of them Super 8 thingies, and this film of my fourth birthday. He was just going to show it when Grant came in, which really put a damper on the party. He said he wanted to see Courtney, but looking back I think it was just an excuse to see me. I let him take her to the Vic so that we could turn the music up. Bianca and Ricky had to leave, too, because she weren't feeling well – stomach cramps or something.

Anyway it was weird to see the film. I remember Dad following us round with this little camera but I don't remember that birthday at all. Mum got all emotional watching it and went out to the kitchen. She was gone ages, so I went to check on her. I overheard her tell Gianni she was leaving Walford. 'What?' I said, 'Are you walking out on us again?' and she went, 'Yes,' cool as a cucumber. I completely lost it and shouted a load of stuff I shouldn't have, then ran out. I felt so angry, so betrayed.

Beppe came after me and was really sweet, and I ended up going back to his place. He listened to me rabbiting on about Mum and poured brandy down me throat and I began to feel a bit better. We started playing this game with his handcuffs. I knew what I was doing. It was me that kissed him. I wanted it to happen. I thought, to hell with everything, I'm gonna go to bed with Beppe and have some fun. But when it came to it, I couldn't. There we was, totally naked, and I've got this gorgeous Italian guy about to make passionate love to me, and all I could think was, 'This feels wrong. It should be Grant.' Beppe was hurt, I could see. He said he loved me. I felt so awful, leading him on like that, but even then he was a real gentleman, lending me his coat cos it was pouring down outside.

I went back to the flat and found Mum packing. She was in as bad a state as me, worse, if anything. I told her not to go, that I didn't mean what I'd said earlier, then I told her I'd made up my mind to go back to Grant. But all of a sudden she was dead against it and threatening to stop me. I said, 'Mum, how you gonna stop me loving him?' Cos that's what it boils down to in the end. It just took another man to prove it to me. She even tried to make out she knew something about Grant, but I told her there was nothing she could tell me about him that I didn't already know. He's my husband. I know him inside out.

I've never seen Grant so apologetic. He was begging my forgiveness almost before I'd set foot in the room. I knew then that I'd made the right decision, and that he meant what he said the other day about loving me. I told him I wanted to give it one last try, not just for Courtney but for me, too. At first, he didn't say anything, and for a few seconds I thought I'd read him wrong. I was on the point of leaving, when he whispered, 'No, don't go,' and took my hand. We held each other so tight I could hardly breathe. It was like we'd got to the edge of this great black yawning pit and stared down into it, then stepped back just in time to save ourselves.

15 September 1998

Me and Courtney's back in the Vic again. Poor little kid don't know whether she's coming or going. Still, she seems quite happy, and Grant and Peggy are making a huge fuss of her, which she loves. Grant's so crazy about her, he's like a dog with two tails! Him and me's being gentle with each other at the moment. We haven't been physical or anything, we just cuddle and talk. It's really nice. He's different. I can't quite put my finger on it, but it's like something's happened to change him – for the better.

Mum was really off about me moving back. She left me this note, saying she couldn't bear to see me leave and she was gonna miss me. I mean, I'll only be round the corner! My heart was in me mouth when I read it cos I thought she was gonna do a runner after all, even though I'd persuaded her to stay. She's in a right miserable mood at the moment, going on about having no job and no future and being over the hill. I'm doing me best to buck her up, but it's hard work.

I've got some other good news too. Well, I hope it is. Bianca's pregnant. She's already four months gone, but she didn't find out until Sunday. That was what her stomach cramps were – the baby kicking! She told me everything was fine, so I assumed she'd already had the tests – I mean, after last time, she can't afford to take any chances. Then, today, I was talking about it and Frank laid into me and said I shouldn't be spreading it around until we know whether the baby's gonna be OK. Turns out B's only having her scan today. So why didn't she tell me? I felt a right idiot.

28 September 1998

I'm so excited! There's this swish new health farm opening up and they've offered me the chance to get some work experience doing massages – and I can take a guest! I heard about it from one of the girls on my course cos we all keep in touch. I wrote off and the manager replied almost straight away. It's at short notice, but Grant's fine about it. He said if it was going to benefit my career, I should go. He's really making an effort these days. I feel a bit bad about dumping Courtney on him for a week, but Peggy and Mum have both promised to lend a hand, so he should be alright. I'm gonna take B with me – she needs a break, she looks absolutely wiped out. I know she's worrying cos she refused to have the scan in the end so they don't know if the baby's got spina bifida or not. She says she's gonna have the baby whatever, so she don't need to have tests. I really admire her for that. But I don't think I could do it.

2 October 1998

We're here, at the health farm. Bianca and Ricky are with me – B wanted to make the most of her time with him before the baby comes along! Simon's running the stall, so she knows it's in safe hands.

I did five massages today. I was a bit nervous to start with, but once I got going, everything was fine. Well, put it this way – no one's complained – yet! It's pretty knackering work actually. I'm dead on me feet this evening and my arms feel as if they're gonna drop off. I expect I'll get used to it after a couple of days. It's really weird to be treated as a professional person. I've been pulling pints in the Vic for so long that I'd begun to think I wasn't capable of doing anything else. But now I know that I've really got something to offer and that people value my opinion, I feel like a new woman!

9 October 1998

Finished at the health farm – and we're now at the seaside! It's a bit quiet, being end of season, but we're having a laugh walking on the beaches and doing all the touristy stuff. It was B's idea – she fancied turning it into a proper holiday. I think it's just what we all need. I phoned Grant and asked him to come up and join us with Courtney. At first I thought he wasn't going to cos he said he was too busy, but then he phoned me back yesterday and said they was on their way. I was so pleased to see Courtney again. I hate being parted from her, even for a night. Grant's not said much, but I think that's because we're with Bianca and Ricky. B's hardly Grant's favourite person (the feeling's mutual there) and she can gab for England, that girl. I'm surprised Ricky ever gets a word in. Come to think of it, he don't!

16 October 1998

It's really nice having this time away together as a family. We're having such fun with Courtney, seeing everything through her eyes – it's like being kids ourselves. It's all so new and strange for her. Her face when she tried my candyfloss was a picture, and when we put her on this little kiddies' ride at the funfair, her eyes were like saucers. She was sitting up so straight, holding on to the bar, all solemn, then she got her confidence and started waving and bouncing up and down with this huge grin. Grant won a teddy bear for her in the shooting gallery and she takes it with her everywhere, even though it's almost as big as she is. He's taken about a million photos of her already. I think I know who his favourite girl is – I don't get much of a look-in these days.

Actually, it's beginning to get to me. Not the time he spends with Courtney, I'd never begrudge him that, but how little time he spends alone with me. It's almost as if he's avoiding being close. We haven't argued, so I suppose that's something, but it's as if he's somewhere else in his head. And we still haven't made love, either. A month without nookie! I'm starting to think he don't fancy me any more.

22 October 1998

Got home earlier today. The Vic's been jumping all evening – Peggy and Frank announced they was getting engaged and cracked open a case of champagne. Phil and Grant were in a right old stink about it. They reckon Frank's just doing it to get his hands on the Vic. I said to Grant, 'What's wrong with him marrying her because he likes her?' But he just went, 'What – at their age?' That's the trouble with Grant, he always thinks people have got ulterior motives. He was having a gloat later because Frank disappeared and Peggy got in a strop and told Grant the engagement was off. I dunno what went on, but then she disappeared, too. They came back really late and went straight upstairs. Their bedroom door was shut when I went past, so I guess it's all on again now…

5 November 1998

Bonfire night. I didn't take Courtney out – she's too young for all those loud bangs, it would only frighten her. We watched some of the fireworks from the living-room window, though. She liked that. The council had a proper display and a bonfire, lots of people went from here. I saw Steven, Peter and Lucy, Ian Beale's children, all wrapped up in their woolly hats. They looked really excited about it.

Course, the sirens were going all night too, and we heard one really close by. It turned out the old folks' flats had gone up in smoke. Peggy went out and found the residents shivering in the community centre and brought them all in here. She's been having a ball, doling out brandies and talking about the 'blitz spirit'. Poor old Dot Cotton's one of them. Alex has taken her back to the vicarage, along with some of the others.

Me and Grant were having a few fireworks of our own because I'd arranged this really special night out for us up West on Saturday, and then I found out him and Phil were going to football instead. I was really fed up until Grant said he was gonna cancel it with Phil. I made sure he did, too. Our love life needs help and a West End show followed by a candlelit dinner might just do the trick.

6 November 1998

Shock news. Cindy Beale's dead. She died in childbirth in prison, apparently. Pat told us the news today. I never knew her that well, but I feel quite cut up about it. You just don't think of people your own age dying, do you? And whatever she did to Ian, she always loved her kids. The thought of them growing up without a mummy – especially the little baby – really upsets me.

17 November 1998

Well, I've got me massage business up and running at long last – no thanks to some people round here. The stupid jokes and comments I've had to put up with…Gianni was really nasty. He took one of my cards and said he'd put it in the phone box. Barry Evans was no better, making cracks about Swedish body rubs and 'Nurse Tiff's Cure-All', which got all the blokes in the Vic sniggering. At least Grant stuck up for me, which makes a change. He knows I'm serious about this. I've done a deal with the bloke who hires out the community centre. There's a room there that's perfect – just the right size. I'm starting next week. Can't wait!

I ran into Beppe yesterday, on the way to get my posters printed. Haven't seen him around much lately, I think he must have been avoiding me. It was a bit awkward, to be honest. He said he was going away on holiday, and when I asked him if he was taking anyone with him, he said, 'There's no one else I'd want to take. No one who isn't married with children.' His eyes looked really sad. I still feel bad about what I did to him.

20 November 1998

Our anniversary yesterday totally bombed. We was going to go to this really exclusive restaurant – you usually see pictures of celebs coming out of it in the Sunday papers – but that was before I discovered Grant had been discussing our sex life (or lack of) with Phil. After that, I just wasn't in the mood for poncing about – or anything else for that matter. To cap it all, Grant's anniversary present to me was this pair of lacy tart's knickers – I mean, talk about heavy hint, it practically made a hole in the floor. Grant ordered a meal to be delivered to us instead, and we did light some candles, but even that didn't work. Courtney kept waking up with the snuffles and she wouldn't settle back into her cot. I was pacing the floor with her for ages and the food got cold. In the end, I took her to bed with us, though none of us got a very good night's sleep. There ain't a lot you can do with a baby in between you. I have to admit that, secretly, I was glad of the excuse. I don't know why, but something's making me hold back. I feel Grant's hand on my skin and I freeze. I want to get back to how we were, but I don't know how.

23 November 1998

I thought I'd really blown it today. I've been so focused on get-ting my business up and running that I didn't realise how hard Grant was trying to support me. It was my first morning at work today and I was full of it because I got five clients. Five! That's really good for a start, and none of them was dodgy blokes in macs, either. Anyway, Grant came to meet me at lunch and wanted me to come back to the Vic, but I'd promised Ricky that I'd talk to Bianca, so I turned him down. Trouble is, B wants a home birth, which would be fine under normal circumstances, but no one knows how this pregnancy's gonna pan out. Ricky's terrified about the risk to the baby, but B just won't listen to him and he don't want to upset her even more. I told her she was being a bully – which I can see now was putting it a bit strong – and she went off in a mega-huff. When I got back, Grant had a go at me, accusing me of putting Bianca before him, which was the last straw.

It made me do something really stupid. I went over to Beppe's. He'd left this good luck card for me this morning, taped to the door of the community centre. It said, 'Be what you want to be. Beppe. XXX.' It's like he's the only one who really understands. Whereas Grant seems to have this idea of what he wants me to be and that I'm supposed to conform to. Anyway, I asked Beppe to take me out for a drive and he did, though he was a bit surprised. Then we stopped in a lane and I kissed him. I knew the second I'd done it what a cruel and selfish thing it was to do. Beppe's so sweet and sympathetic and I was just using him to prop myself up because I was feeling bad. I just said, 'I'm sorry,' and got out the car and ran off. Luckily I managed to find a taxi to get home.

Me and Grant didn't speak to each other again until after closing. I was feeling even worse by then cos Frank had told me all about the steak lunch and the card Grant had got me. I said, 'I haven't been doing a lot of listening lately, have I?' and Grant said, 'You've started a business up and I'm really proud of that.' I was taken aback cos I thought he hated it, but he admitted the reason he's been touchy is because he's scared I'm gonna become a big success and leave him. I think both of us admitting that we weren't perfect broke the barriers down. We kissed and suddenly it felt so right that I knew what I wanted to do next. I'll give you a clue. It wasn't crochet!

I've been kicking myself over Beppe, but things are so much better with Grant now and I'm terrified of ruining it. We're really happy – it's like being on our holiday in Paris all over again, we can't keep our hands off each other. I couldn't bear the thought of messing that up now, after all we've been through. It's taken so long to get here. Unfortunately, Beppe's been asking after me with Frank, and then today I ran into him in the Square. He was pretty narked about the other day and asked what I was playing at, shooting off like that. I apologised and said it was just a moment of weakness, which didn't go down too well, either.

But Phil must've seen us and told Grant cos when I got back to the Vic he had worked up a real head of steam. I realised then that I had to be honest with him. If there's one thing both of us should have learned by now, it's that lies only trip you up in the end. So I told Grant it was my fault, that I'd kissed Beppe because I thought Grant didn't care about me any more. Of course, he went storming off to sort Beppe out and I sat there biting me nails for the next half-hour, waiting for the sound of sirens or something. But when he came back in he was quite calm and said he hadn't touched Beppe. Then he went, 'I don't suppose it matters much now. It's over with him, isn't it?' I could feel the relief washing over me in waves. I said, 'It was never anything to begin with,' and he seemed OK with that. Mind you, I'm still pinching meself. Maybe Grant was abducted by aliens while he was outside and a clone came back in instead. Don't know how else to explain his behaviour... I thought he was gonna kill me!

30 November 1998

Today started off so well. Up until about an hour ago I think it was the best day of my life. But since then, it's been the absolute worst.

I almost knew it was too good to be true when Grant bought me the dress. It was this fantastic designer number, absolutely to die for. We were going out for a meal – Grant's idea, he wanted to make up for all the rotten times we've had – and he'd gone and got the dress specially this afternoon. I was so touched I started crying. I just felt so happy. Not because of the dress, but because Grant's been so wonderful. Everything was going brilliantly, it was like a dream come true. He never stopped kissing me and saying lovely things and he was so passionate and tender with me in bed. It was like, 'What if I'm never this happy again?' Like when you're so full to the brim with happiness you think you're gonna burst.

We went out to this really posh French restaurant, all stiff linen napkins and waiters with little dickie bows. Grant drank a toast to me – 'For showing me how to love someone again,' he said. I knew then that he really did mean it, at last, and that it was me he wanted, not Sharon. He didn't really want to talk about her, but I said, 'Come on, Grant. Let's get all the skeletons out of the cupboard.' He opened up and said how Phil and Sharon's affair had torn him apart. They'd been really happy up till then and were even planning on having a baby. I know how badly that must have hurt him, but when I asked if he wished he'd never found out, he said no, cos if it hadn't happened he'd never have met me or had Courtney.

I said, 'So what's changed? What's made you fall in love with me?' and he was completely honest. He said, 'I suppose I've always thought I wanted something else, but it was a fantasy. You're the one who's real.' Then he started on about all the little things he loves about me, like how patient I am with Courtney and how he loves hearing me sing in the bath! He said, 'I feel like I've been living with you all this time without ever really being there. We've never had that first time most people have, when everything's perfect. You and me, we've still got that to look forward to. That's where we are now.'

It was like he was giving me all of himself, every last little bit. No more secrets, no more lies, all that stuff in the past finally laid to rest. And I wanted to give him all of me in return. I knew there was one gift we would both treasure and suddenly it felt like the right time. I said, 'Grant, you know when you asked me about what I really wanted? Well, I'd like to try for another baby.' He was over the moon about it and so was I. We were both so high I think we floated home cos I'm sure my feet didn't touch the ground...and then I came crashing down to earth again.

I heard them on the baby monitor. Grant and Mum. He'd gone up to check on Courtney and Mum must've followed him. I was still in the bar and I saw the little lights flashing on the parents unit. I thought Courtney must be screaming, so I took it out into the hall where it was quieter and turned up the volume. I heard Grant tell Mum how much he loved me and that he shuddered to think how close he'd come to wrecking my life. I even smiled at that. Then I heard Mum say, 'We both did. But if you care about her as much as you say you do, why were we nearly kissing the other night?' He went, 'Because there's something between us, you know there is,' and she said, 'Don't give me that. You just used me for sex while she wasn't giving you any, and now that she is, you want me for babysitting instead.' My hand was trembling so much I could hardly hold the intercom. Then I heard Grant say, 'Look, Louise, what we had was amazing. I've never wanted anyone so much. You wanted it as much as I did,' and Mum was agreeing and saying how exciting it was.

I was shaking all over by then and I dropped the thing on the floor. If they'd stabbed me through the heart, they couldn't have hurt me more. Betrayed by my mother and my husband. The two people I loved most in the world. I feel disgusted, physically sick. I'm still shaking. I can't stop. One minute my world was complete, now it's shattered into tiny pieces. I don't know what to do, it's as if my brain's seized up. The minutes creep past and I'm sitting here on the sofa in the dark, holding Courtney close to me, wondering if this terrible night will ever end. All I do know is I can't stay here any more. I never want to see either of them ever again.

21 December 1998

I feel as if I've been somewhere far away, but I don't know where. Everything's still pretty hazy. I'm in hospital. My chest is sore and I've got bandages round my head. I came round yesterday, and for a few seconds I thought I must be dead because I didn't know where I was or how I'd got there. I remember thinking that heaven looked like quite an ordinary sort of place and not so scary after all, then these faces swam into view and I recognised Bianca and Simon and Dad.

Apparently, the first thing I did was ask where Grant was, though I don't remember that. Bianca told me this morning, when she came round by herself. She said he wasn't allowed near me because the police thought he was the one who'd hurt me. Seems I fell down the stairs in the Vic and they think he pushed me. Then she started talking about Grant having an affair and she asked if I remembered anything. And that was when it started to come back about what him and Mum had done.

The police came round later while Simon was here. This detective was asking me all these questions, but I said my mind was a blank. After they'd left I was gonna tell Simon, but I just couldn't. I couldn't bring myself to say the words, 'Our mother slept with Grant.' But I am starting to remember the rest. It's coming back, bit by bit, brief flashes which don't seem to be in any order. The nurse said I shouldn't push myself too hard, it's my memory's way of protecting me from the trauma.

Bianca told me about my injuries. She said I had cracked ribs and a collapsed lung and if the paramedics hadn't got to me when they did I would have died. Then they found out I had a blood clot on the brain and I had to have surgery and I've been in intensive care on life support ever since. No one knew whether I was gonna pull through or whether I'd be brain damaged or what.

I can hardly take it in. I was that close to death – twice. Actually, it was three times according to B, cos Grant and Beppe had a fight by my bed and dislocated the machine that was helping me breathe. That's why my family got a court order taken out to stop Grant coming near me. I'm so relieved. I couldn't bear to see him again.

23 December 1998

Peggy came in today, with Courtney. Ahh, it was so wonderful to see my little baby. I held her in my arms and buried my face in her hair and just drank in her smell. She patted my cheek and gave me this naughty little grin and was about to start bouncing all over me when Peggy whisked her off, which was just as well cos my ribs are still sore.

Course, Peggy was trying to defend Grant and was going on about how he wouldn't have hurt me deliberately and that the affair was probably a stupid mistake (everyone knows Grant had another woman because Bianca broadcast it in the Vic). I was about to put her straight about Grant's 'mistake' when Mum walked in. I think Peggy sensed a bit of an atmosphere cos she left straight away.

As for Mum, I didn't give her time to draw breath. She was pathetic, trying to apologise and telling me she loved me. After what she's done! I said I'd sooner forgive Grant than her. She went to touch me and I whacked her across the face as hard as I could. I told her I didn't want her filthy, stinking, cheating hands anywhere near me ever again. I said, 'I never want to hear from you, I never want to see you. As far as I'm concerned, you're dead. You do not exist.' She went out crying and I kept thinking, 'Good, I hope you suffer, cos you'll never suffer as much as I have and it ain't never gonna go away for me, neither.'

24 December 1998

What a place to spend Christmas Eve. The doctors said I might be able to go home tomorrow, though. Home, that's a laugh, innit? Where I am going to go? I asked Simon if I could stop at his place. He was a bit surprised that I didn't want to go over to Mum's for Christmas dinner, but I said I wanted to spend some time with B. She and Ricky have split up over this home birth business with the baby and she really needs me, so at least that's not a lie.

Si thinks Grant pushed me. They all do. It wouldn't take much to get Grant arrested – Bianca's already made a statement about last Christmas, and Phil's godson, Jamie, heard us fighting. Simon said I should tell the police and get Grant put safely behind bars. That way, he wouldn't be able to get his hands on me or Courtney. I don't know whether I can, though. It wouldn't be true. The DCI came back later and interviewed me again, but I stuck to my story about not remembering. He knows I'm hiding something, and he's right. But it's not what he thinks, I just can't tell anyone about Grant and Mum.

See, I remember it all perfectly now. The day it happened, I was gonna leave Grant and run away to Italy with Beppe. I found out he was going on holiday with Little Joe and I asked him to take me and Courtney with him. He'd told me he'd be there if I ever needed him, and he was as good as his word. I managed to get Grant out the way with some story about picking up a prescription for Courtney, and while he was gone I stuffed a load of our clothes into a laundry bag and hauled it over to Bianca's. We talked about Grant having an affair, but I didn't tell her who with. She helped me pack a holdall and we said our goodbyes, then I bundled Courtney into Beppe's car.

We was just about to leave when I realised I didn't have my passport. I went flying back to the Vic but it took me ages to find it because it had fallen down the side of the bed. I'd just found it and had turned to go when Grant appeared in the doorway. I told him our marriage was over, that I knew about him and Mum, and that I was leaving him and taking Courtney. He was so stunned that I was able to get past him before he could do anything about it. I was at the top of the stairs when he caught up with me. We had this tussle and he grabbed hold of my arm and I screamed at him to take his hands off me. He said, 'Not until we talk about this,' and I said, 'You'll have to kill me first,' and yanked my arm away. I was off-balance and the next thing I knew I was falling and there was nothing I could do to save myself. Then it all went dark. I don't remember anything else till I came round a few days ago...

9.30pm: I've done it. Shopped Grant. I had to. He came in here today and scared the life outta me. As soon as I saw him, I reached for the alarm button, but he grabbed hold of me before I could get to it. He told me he wasn't gonna hurt me and to stay calm. It made me feel like a hostage or something. I said I was going to divorce him and get custody of Courtney and he said he'd fight me if I did. I said he'd lose then, because I'd tell everyone he knocked me down the stairs. I meant it, too. There's no way he's going anywhere near my daughter again and I'll do whatever it takes to stop him, even lie. It's no less than he's done, after all. Then I made another dive for the panic button and this time I got there. He gave me this look and for a second I thought he was gonna rip me to pieces, then he turned and ran out the room. Beppe came in a few seconds later and asked me what had happened. And that's when I told him my memory had come back.

25 December 1998

Came out today. Beppe picked me up. I still wasn't sure about making a statement at that point. Like I said to Beppe, 'He's not getting a parking ticket, we're talking about attempted murder.' I rang Grant and asked for Courtney cos I was desperate to see her, but he said I wasn't having her and hung up. That was what decided me. I told Beppe to drive me to the police station. We passed Bianca on the way and I told her about Courtney and she said she'd go round after dinner and get her off Grant. I wasn't sure about it, Bianca being nearly eight months pregnant and all, but she insisted and I wasn't gonna say no, was I?

I arranged to meet her back at Pat's at two, but when we got there Bianca hadn't returned from the Vic. I left it as long as I dared, but by five o'clock there was still no sign of her and I was beginning to get this awful sick feeling in my stomach. Then, just as we was crossing the road, an ambulance drew up outside the Vic. I feared the worst, I really did, but it was OK. B had gone into labour five weeks early and she'd had the baby in the pub. It's a bonny little boy. Ricky was there, too, grinning from ear to ear.

I couldn't believe it when B told me Grant had helped deliver it. She said he was brilliant. I was starting to regret what I'd done, but by then it was too late. A police car came round the corner and DCI Mason got out and arrested Grant. He was shouting, 'I didn't do it, I didn't do it. Tell him, Tiff.' I couldn't bear to stay in the same room, I felt such a traitor. I picked up Courtney and ran outside and got into Beppe's car, hugging Courtney to me so she wouldn't see Grant being led away. I didn't feel good about it like I thought I would. I hated myself.

28 December 1998

Me and Courtney's staying at Simon's at the moment. I can't relax though. I'm as jumpy as a kitten, expecting Grant to come barging through the door at any moment. It's stupid, I know – I mean, he's been denied bail, so it ain't possible – but I can't help it.

I still feel completely awful, like I've been through the wringer, sort of squeezed dry of emotion. Beppe's being really kind, but I'm worried about him too – he wants more than I can give. He's been acting like I'm his girlfriend, kissing and cuddling me and wanting to take me out, but I don't feel that way about him. I just don't know how to tell him after everything he's done for me.

Went to see Bianca today and the baby. He's a gorgeous little thing. She's a natural as a mother, you can see it straight off. Her and Ricky are on better terms, thank goodness. I know they'll be alright, those two. They were made for each other. Not like me and Grant... Silly thing is, I really thought him and me were made for each other too. If I hadn't overheard Grant and Mum talking, I'd still think that. Him and me'd be living in wedded bliss, Courtney would still have a dad, I'd still have a mum and Grant wouldn't be in prison. We might all have lived happily ever after. Stranger things have happened. But now I'll never know whether it would have worked out or not. Anyway, there's no point in thinking about it. I don't love Grant any more. It feels like something's just gone out of me. I loved him for three years and now I don't. End of story.

Do I wish I hadn't found out? No. We'd have been living a lie and it would have come out eventually, then I'd've been even more let down than I am now. And at least Courtney's too young to understand or remember any of this, whereas if she was older... well, I remember how I felt when my parents split up. I don't want her to go through that.

30 December 1998

I've made up my mind. Me and Courtney are leaving. I've booked us tickets to Spain. One-way. We fly on New Year's

Day. I've got friends over there, contacts in the beauty business, I know the country, I like the people. We'll make a new life for ourselves away from here. I'll miss Simon, and I'll miss Bianca and Ricky and seeing their baby grow up, but they can all come and visit. I'll miss Beppe, too, of course. He's been so good to me. I wish it could've worked out. In many ways he was ideal, but the spark just wasn't there. Not for me, anyway.

I won't miss anyone else, apart from Peggy, maybe. She's been more of a mother to me than Mum ever was. As for Mum, I pity her because I've got something she'll never have – a daughter. And no matter what happens, how lonely or scared I get, I will never, ever do to Courtney what she's done to me over the years. That's why I can't forgive her. There's just no excuse for betraying your own like that.

Courtney's my life now and I'm gonna give her everything I can. I'm getting quite excited about it. I'm only 22, I've got my whole future ahead of me. You never know, I still might land that millionaire with a yacht! And if I don't, I know I can make it on my own. Being with Grant's taught me that, at least. In a funny way, he's given me the power to set myself free cos if it weren't for him, I wouldn't be as strong as I am now. Strong enough to walk away from him, at last.

Postscript

by Bianca Butcher

1 January 1999

That was the last entry in Tiffany's diary. She was killed early this morning, a few seconds into the New Year, knocked down by a car in Albert Square. Frank was driving, but it was as much Grant's fault. If he hadn't been trying to snatch Courtney, Tiffany wouldn't have run out into the road after him and she'd still be here today. Or, rather, she'd be on a plane, off to start her new life away from Grant and all the misery he brought her.

I think, somewhere in the back of my mind, I always knew he'd kill her. Only not like this, in a pool of blood in a dark, cold street. I was right by her when she died. She couldn't speak, she just looked up at Courtney, who was in Grant's arms, like she was checking she was OK, then sank back. Something seemed to go out of her eyes, like a light had been switched off. I went with her in the ambulance, holding her hand, but it was too late.

We said our goodbyes yesterday, when she came over to see me and Harry (our new baby). Tiff brought a bottle of bubbly and we sat and nattered about the old days, when we was at school together. We had a giggle, but I could tell she was sad underneath. She said she wished it had all turned out differently with her and Grant. I told her she'd given him every chance and then some. But that's Tiff, innit? Soft as lights. She gave me a letter to give to the police after she'd gone to Spain. I said, 'It's about Grant, innit?' But she went, 'It's better if you don't know.'

I wanted her to go and get Courtney off Peggy, see the New Year in with me and Ricky. If she had...well, I wouldn't be writing this now. I still don't know how Grant got out – they must have given him bail after all. I know she visited him in prison yesterday and told him she was going away with Courtney, but both of us thought he was safely locked up.

I was too choked up when she left to say what I really wanted to say – how much I loved her. All I said was, 'You're me best mate. What am I gonna do without you?' We hugged each other and cried and she said if I ever needed her, to let her know. That was Tiff all over – warm, generous, kind. She had a heart of gold, that girl. And there was something else about Tiff, I mean, besides being gorgeous and funny and smart. She was a spark of pure life. I've seen it loads of times – she'd walk into a room and set it buzzing. I just can't believe that spark's gone out. I can't believe she's gone.

Tiffany only told me about this diary recently, when she was in hospital. She asked me to get it for her and bring it in. So I did. She swore me to secrecy, said she didn't want Grant to find out what was in it. That's why I went over to Simon's today and took it out of her suitcase. I'm keeping it safe for Courtney. One day, when she's old enough to understand, I'll give this to her. I want her to know what a wonderful mother she had and how much she loved her. Even though Tiff won't be there, she's alive, in these pages. She can tell her herself.

TIFFANY'S SECRET DIARY
Members of the cast who appear in the pictures.

Tiffany Mitchell	Martine McCutcheon
Grant Mitchell	Ross Kemp
Simon Raymond	Andrew Lynford
Bianca Butcher	Patsy Palmer
Tony Hills	Mark Homer
Phil Mitchell	Steve McFadden
Peggy Mitchell	Barbara Windsor
Kathy Mitchell	Gillian Taylforth
Ricky Butcher	Sid Owen
Diane Butcher	Sophie Lawrence
Terry Raymond	Gavin Richards
Irene Raymond	Roberta Taylor
Beppe di Marco	Michael Greco
Gianni di Marco	Marc Bannerman
Louise Raymond	Carol Harrison

THE AUTHOR

Kate Lock was born in Oxford, where she grew up and began her career as a journalist on the *Oxford Star*. She moved to London, where she worked for *Radio Times* for six years and she continues to write for the magazine on a freelance basis. She has written three other novelisations: Jimmy McGovern's *The Lakes* (as K.M. Lock) for BBC/Penguin, *Where the Heart Is: Home* (Headline) and *Blood Ties: The Life and Loves of Grant Mitchell* (BBC). Kate lives in York with her husband Stephen and daughter Isis.